EDWARD'S CAT.

THE RISE OF THE KITTENS. AND A DOG

BOOK TWO

MARIA P FRINO

MPG COMMUNICATIONS

Book Two

Edward's Cat. The Rise of the Kittens. And a Dog.

Maria P Frino

This is a work of fiction.

Title: Edward's Cat. The Rise of the Kittens. And a Dog– a novella

Author: Maria P. Frino

Cover Design: Mark Drolc - http://onthemarkdesign.com.au/

Visit the author's website at www.mariapfrino.com

All inquiries should be made to the author - mariapfrino@gmail.com

 Created with Vellum

CHAPTER 1

Edward
Logan the Kitten

I'm standing with other parents in the school playground. A misery of humans, huddled, hunched, and wet. Our golf umbrellas are only helping the top half of our bodies. Even though the storm has passed, the wind is still whipping up the rain, our legs are soaked. And isn't it fun standing in wet feet?

Some lucky parents managed to scramble undercover, others pull rain gear around them to minimise being soaked. Why do we get a storm right on three o'clock when it is time for school pick up?

As all this is happening, the children start bolting out of classrooms heading straight towards their parents. But where's Logan? My parent brain goes straight to thinking something bad has happened.

Next thing, I look down at my feet and there is a kitten,

a very wet kitten, looking up at me. "What? Where did you come ... oh, is that you Logan?

"Yes, Daddy. What is going on?"

I understand what he is saying but anyone else around would have heard a tortured meow. Picking him up I head towards the car, "I'll explain when we're home, your mother needs to see this."

Heading into our driveway, Sally is outside waiting for us, I had called ahead. The rain is spattering in the wind. "Where is he?"

"I'm here," says Logan as he scampers down onto the wet path with a meow.

"Oh, Logan. Look at you." Sally scoops him up cuddling him into her. "You're big for a kitten."

"He's a Maine Coon, they're the largest domestic cat in the world. Come on, let's get inside and dry off."

"Thanks for the lesson, Edward. I did know that." She smiles, "he's still very cute. Look how bright his green eyes are as a kitten."

I'm behind them as we enter our home and the heating hits me first, then the heady smell of baked goods. Sally must have come home early from her job as a Librarian. Our little semi-detached house is cosy, decorated in an eclectic mix of Sally's antique stall buys and my tech para-phernalia. Things are mismatched and colourful suiting our lifestyle, which is hectic yet homely.

"When I heard it was going to storm, I came home to bring in the washing. Then I thought you two may come home wet, so I baked a chocolate cake."

"Thanks Mummy, yum. Can cats eat cake?"

Sally and I laugh. "You're not going to remain a cat, Logan. And no, they can't."

"I guess we should explain what has happened to you," I say as Logan stares up with his bright green kitten eyes. "You already know about our secret, the fact we are magicals, you included. What we didn't know is what magic you were going to have. So, it looks like you can transform into a cat like me."

"Like the magic Aunty Milly gave you. That's secret too. I haven't told anybody, I promise." As Logan the Cat is meowing this, he is back to being the human form of Logan.

"Welcome back." Logan hops onto a dining chair, his blonde locks limp, his bum still damp. "That's right, we've explained about me and Aunt Milly, she was the only magical in my family who then passed on her magic to me when she died. You've been born with the magic so we are a family of three magicals, something that is to stay still a secret and only shared with people we trust. Like your grandparents."

"Wow, we are special, Daddy."

"Not special, Logan," says Sally, "we are given powers that non-magicals don't possess and we use them wisely. Non-magicals are suspicious of magic because they align it with the occult." Logan gives Sally a querying look.

"What your mother is talking about when she says *occult*, is dark, evil magic, magic that can cause problems for non-magicals. That's not what we're about. We use our magic to help non-magicals if and when necessary."

"Oh, so we're superheroes. Wow, that is so cool."

Both Sally and I laugh loving Logan's enthusiasm, "You could say that."

Sally offers us some cake and hot chocolate, which on a cold July day is perfect.

We're all sitting at the dining table with Logan having asked many questions while devouring the cake. "You're only six, Logan, so for now let's leave it that you know you will transform into Logan the Cat at times. We don't know whether you will have control of when this happens, but ..."

Sally interrupts, "He won't. Control doesn't happen until he's a teenager. The only saving grace is that before then he won't transform often. He will be a mature cat by the time he can control when and where he transforms."

"Oh, right," I say with a mouthful of the delicious cake, "that's the part I had to learn how to do because I inherited Milly's magic. My sister unfortunately neglected to give me the control."

Sally looks at me, "And you're still dirty about that? Let it go, Edward, she probably wasn't able to give you control, that's something we'll never know. You have it now and that's all that matters."

I look forlorn but know she is right. Still, I'm jealous of the fact she and Logan were born with their powers.

"Is it ok to go to my room? My friends are waiting for me on the computer. I've finished. It was delicious, thanks Mummy."

Both of us nod and watch as he heads upstairs. I am amazed at how Logan remembers his manners, something Sally has drilled into him.

Sally wipes a tear from her eye, "Our little boy is growing up. Who knows what is ahead of him." I reach over and take her hand, squeezing it. I smile knowing we are both worried about how he will deal with this new stage of his life.

We're in bed. I'm listening to Sally's contended sleeping noises next to me. I can't sleep. Our little boy discovering he is a magical has brought back memories of when I was bestowed my powers. Unlike Sally and Logan, I wasn't born a magical, my powers were inherited from my twin sister, Milly, when she passed away of cancer at the tender age of ten. A tear makes its way down my cheek, tickling it with memories of her. She is always with me even though I haven't used my powers since leaving school … well, only once or twice when it has been absolutely necessary.

I think about how far I've come from those turbulent days of being bullied and forming the geek gang with Trudi, who is still my best friend and who married her best friend, Jackson. I laugh to myself how ironic that is because Jackson was a bully until he came to our side.

Many things have changed, not the least is I'm now on the committee of the A-Alliance, the secret magical society that protects all magicals.

I yawn. I press the button on my phone, which is still in my hand because I had been scrolling aimlessly until my reminiscing took me away from it. It's 2am, I yawn again. Placing my phone on the side table, I put my head down still thinking of my twin, missing her doesn't seem to be any easier now I'm an adult. Sleep finally arrives as I then think of Logan and what is ahead of him.

CHAPTER 2

LOGAN
The School Bullies

Chloe, my sort-of cousin, started school this year. Uncle Jackson and Aunty Trudi are my Mummy and Daddy's friends, Chloe is their daughter. I'm in Year 1 and she's in Kindy. I like protecting her and she likes having me around.

My daddy met my uncle and aunty at high school. I like that they are friends, and also my daddy's other friends, Athena and Nigel. I like playing with their daughter, Ailsa. I can say her name properly now but when I was little I called her Als. We all still call her by that nickname. Als is two years older than me and is in Year 3. We both look after Chloe and our parents' call us the *Terrific Trio*. Chloe can transform like me, but Als is a non-magical so we don't talk about our magic in front of her. We know we have to keep it secret.

Speaking of keeping our magic secret, I like that I have this amazing power because I feel special, I have a superpower. What is bad about it is I am being bullied and can't control when I can transform and fight back like my daddy did when he was at school. Daddy has told me stories of how he and Aunty Trudi asked others who were bullied to join them. They formed a type of club to fight the bullies helping to have the rules changed at school. This school has zero-tolerance to bullying now. My parents have explained to me what that means – the school will not allow bullying of any kind, but the bullies still try because they don't follow rules.

Alex and Callum, two big Year 4 boys, are walking towards us as we head out of the school gate to wait for my daddy to pick us up. "Hey, losers, we have something to talk about."

I hear Alex yelling this and watch terrified, my body shaking, as they walk towards us. "Stay calm," I say to Chloe and Als knowing I'm shaking more than they are.

"Where the hell did you disappear to Logan? The other day when we all saw the kitten in the playground." Alex and Callum are in front of us now stopping us walking any further.

The street is full of buses taking kids home. Teachers are making sure kids get on the right bus. Busy parents wait in cars. Other kids are walking like we are. I don't think these two are going to try something stupid with so many people around.

"What?" I look Alex straight in the eye even though fear is gripping my body. I'm trembling inside and breathe in deep. The girls are standing behind me, Chloe having whispered she will scream if needed.

"Don't play dumb with me, where were you?"

"I was picked up by my father. I don't know what you're talking about." As I say this I hear my name called, daddy is waiting for us across the road. "We have to go, bye Alex, bye Callum." I breathe a sigh of relief as we head towards where daddy is parked, he's in his beat-up old Ute he uses for work, he's a builder.

"Sorry guys, I was held up at work so couldn't go home to get the clean car, you'll have to squeeze in I'm afraid." Daddy was talking about our other car, a sedan that would have been more comfortable, not bumpy and squeezy like this one. Lucky the drive to our homes is a short one.

When we're home daddy asks whether we are being bothered by those two bullies.

"Umm, maybe. They wanted to know where I was when the kitten appeared in the playground. I was scared but I looked him in the eyes like you taught me, Daddy."

"Hmm, well done, but be careful around those two, they have a bad reputation."

I wasn't sure what the big word daddy said was, but I know Alex and Callum are bad.

Two days later I'm coming out of the toilet block when Callum shoves me back inside. I fall on the cold, hard floor. "Ow, what did you do that for?"

"We have unfinished business." Alex's disembodied voice booms in from outside as he appears menacingly over the top of me. "What's with you disappearing?"

I try to push myself off the floor only to be shoved again by Alex. "I told you before, I went home with my daddy."

"Oh, poor daddy's boy." He says this in a high-pitched whisper. "There's somethin' strange about you, Logan. Even your name is suss! I'm going to find out, you just watch me." With this he and Callum walk out leaving me on the floor needing to wee again. Well, I'm in the right place.

I head outside ready to play with my friends, it's lunchtime, when they both accost me again before I can reach where Chloe and Als are standing.

"Not so fast, you didn't give me any money this week. Come on, cough it up."

I look at Alex like he has two heads, "I don't have any money. Who brings money anymore when our parents' pay each week." This was part of the no bullying policy the school has where students are not allowed to carry cash. This way bullies can't take what isn't theirs.

"Yeah, I know but you're supposed bring some cash for us. Remember, we have a deal?" What he's saying is true, when students start at this school, they are approached by Alex and Callum who give them assurances that they will be looked after if they pay them a weekly sum. There are other bullies at this school, but these two are the worst.

I really want to be rid of them so I say, "Ok, I'll bring you some money tomorrow. Now, please let me go to my friends."

Alex bows down and sweeps his arm allowing me to pass. I try not to laugh at how silly he looks.

"How was school today?" This is my Grandmother Elizabeth, who I call Nan. I'm at my grandparents' home because my mummy and daddy are working late today.

"Ok."

"Has the cat go your tongue? Is that all you have to tell me."

I laugh, "You are funny, Nan."

She laughs at her little joke. "Anymore Logan the Cat episodes?"

Nan knows about us being magicals, just like Grandpa and Nanna Vanessa, my daddy's mum, know. But I am still careful who I speak to about our magical family.

"No, only once."

She smiles at me, "Are you sure you're ok? You are unusually quiet."

"Yes, can I go and do my homework now?" She nods but I can see she is worried. Why do adults always worry? They can't solve all our problems.

I walk into the lounge room where my grandfather's desk is and set my laptop onto it. I try and focus on what I need to do rather than think about those idiots, Alex and Callum.

CHAPTER 3

Ailsa

The Protector

I am the tallest in our group, the Terrific Trio. I like this name and whenever anyone asks about our group, I always tell them our name. People usually laugh. Except bullies, I don't tell them this name because they will only make even more fun of us. I especially don't tell Alex, I try to speak to him as little as I can, he is a jerk. With me being in Year 3, I do run into him often in some combined classes, but I avoid talking to him.

I like protecting Logan and Chloe, they are my friends and because I'm the oldest, then it's my job to look after them. In fact, they are like family to me, not just friends. My mother tells me I am like a mother hen looking after her chicks. So, I guess I can consider my two friends my chicks. I laugh as I think of this as we walk into the school gates.

"What's so funny," says Chloe.

"Oh nothing. Listen, I have to go to see Mrs Chapman

about some extra work, see you both at recess." Both Logan and Chloe wave me goodbye as I head in the opposite direction to them.

I knock on the staffroom door where Mrs Chapman asked me to meet her.

"Oh, Ailsa. Give me a minute, I'm coming."

She is soon by my side and is giving me a sheet with extra lessons I can study for Maths and Science, the two subjects I like the best. "I printed this out for you, keep it on your desk at home and do this extra study when you can. You are a good student Ailsa, I know you will do well."

"Thanks, Mrs Chapman. It's nice of you to help me like this."

"Your mother was happy for me to give you extra work, so it's my pleasure. Now, go and take your seat."

We had arrived in our classroom and as I walk to my seat, Alex is glaring at me. He whispers, "Teacher's pet."

I'm sitting under the Jacaranda tree with Logan and Chloe. There are some tables and chairs where we can eat lunch, we are the only students sitting here until those two bullies turn up.

"I gave Callum the money this morning."

"Yeah, I know. Thanks. Na, we're here about somethin' else."

I look both of them up and down, "There's always something else with you two. Leave us alone."

"Not talking to you, your friend Logan is the one I'm talking to. Now, tell me what you're hiding, I know there is something."

Logan stands up and walks towards Alex and Callum, "You heard Ailsa, leave us alone. I am not hiding anything."

Alex picks him up by the collar, "You hidin' behind

your girlfriend, hey Logan? You're a pussy and a lucky one this time. Come on Callum, there are others we can hassle."

After Alex drops his hand from Logan's neck, he rubs where Alex's fist had been. I walk up to him, "Are you crazy, you know they will keep coming back for more. You should have stayed sitting down." My anger grows as he has put us all in danger.

"They have to know that we are not scared of them."

"But we are scared of them," says Chloe joining us. She has tears in her eyes.

I place my arm gently around Chloe's shoulders telling her nothing will happen, the school has rules.

"Oh yeah, like those rules mean anything to bullies."

I am about to answer Logan when the bell goes for us to go back into class.

We're waiting for Logan's grandmother Vanessa to pick us up when those two annoying idiots come up to us again. Alex, skinny with unkempt oily locks, his voice a lazy Irish lilt, has an evil smile on his face. Callum, his sidekick trailing behind him, is stocky with big green eyes and white-blonde hair. He has the potential to be good looking one day when he grows into his big head. Callum's head hangs down, which means trouble is coming.

"Logan, this is drivin' me nuts. You spill what is going on with you or pay."

I can see Logan's anger oozing over his face and know he is going to react. "Stop right now! Alex, you are delusional, Logan is a student at this school just like you. You're looking to start a fight from nothing."

"Shut up, Ailsa. I'm talkin' to Logan, not you. And he knows what I'm talkin' about." With this he moves closer and stands close to Logan, "Don't ya, mate?" Alex looks down his nose at him.

I am so over this menacing behaviour so I push myself between the two of them and push Alex away. He is furious.

"What the f..." He is stopped mid-sentence when Logan's grandmother pulls up. "This isn't over," whispers Alex in a growl as Logan, Chloe and I step into the car.

CHAPTER 4

LOGAN
Magical and Patience

The A-Alliance house is awesome. We are here because my daddy is receiving some sort of prize, usually young children are not allowed in this house. This special day has been set aside for all magical families to attend. To anyone looking at this house from the street, it's an ugly dump. Non-magicals would freak out if they saw what it's like inside. The Jacaranda tree growing inside is beyond amazing and the meadow that stretches out for miles as if it's a long winding road, is full of massive trees, shrubs and animals. What is amazing is none of this can be viewed from the street. It's a truly magical space and only accessible to us magicals.

Chloe and I are having a blast playing with the magical animals and meeting other kids with powers different to ours. We watch on as two of the older kids show us their powers. I'm in awe when one of them can change his squeaky teenage voice into that of an opera singer. What he can use this magic for to help non-magicals, I'm not sure, but it's entertaining. One day he might use this skill to entertain people, who knows?

"Can you do anything else?" I ask with my voice higher than usual. I'm really interested.

"I have other powers but you two are too young, wait till you're a bit older."

"Aww, but I'm seven, I'm old enough."

"Not quite. Wait a few years to learn this magic craft, it is awesome once you get the hang of it."

That's the thing, ever since I changed into that kitten, ragged and wet by rain, all I want is to be able to learn more magic. Now I need to know how long before I can. "Come on Chloe, I need to speak to my mummy or daddy." Chloe places the rabbit she was holding back in the open hutch and follows me.

We make our way through the adults and finally find them. We wait until one of them is no longer talking. Mummy looks at me and asks if I want something.

"Can we talk to you about magic for a bit, please Mummy."

"You've picked the right place to talk about it. What did you want to know?"

I tell her about the boy with the voice magic and she tells she knows who I'm talking about. "Well, he said he has more powers but he wouldn't show us because we're too young. Am I going to have more powers, Mummy? When?"

She asks us to go and find a space to sit down, "Ok, hold on a minute. This is going to take some time." Once we're settled with a milkshake each that mummy grabbed for us, she continues telling us to be patient. "Your powers don't come fully into force until you are a teenager. For some it can be 11 or 12 years, for others it won't be before they turn 15."

"What? But that is so long away."

"Logan, what did I say about being patient? Besides, you can't change the timing of when you will receive all your powers, none of us can. And, some people only have one power, others like that boy will have more than one. Not all powers are useful though." She continues telling us that the magical community is made up of many different types of people with many different forms of magic. "Take your father for instance, his only power is to shape shift into a cat. However, he used this power to fight bullies and that was good use of his magic in helping the non-magicals. Children and teenagers in particular."

She continues by reminding us of why we are at the A-Alliance house today. "Your father has been honoured with an award for changing how schools deal with bullying, he and your Aunt Trudi, who isn't here today because she's a non-magical, formed a group that helped to stop bullying. He will now sit on the A-Alliance Committee and has the power to make decisions that affect all magicals. You should be proud of him."

"I am, Mummy. But it still sucks that we have to wait so long to know how many magical powers we have."

"Keep doing your studies of magic and before you know it, your powers, if there are more, will appear. You already know you can transform into that beautiful Maine Coon."

"Yeah, I guess that's cool. But when will I transform again?"

Mummy laughs. "Patience, my darling. Patience."

We arrive home late and I'm sleepy. Daddy carries me up to my room and he tells me that what I spoke with

Mummy about will happen. "You will receive all the powers you are meant to have when you're ready to handle them. Maybe you might be like Mummy and me, you will only have one power. We won't know until you are older."

I yawn. A big, huge one. "Ok, Daddy. I had fun today and am proud of you getting that award." Daddy always tells me how proud he is of me, I like that word.

"Thanks," smiles Daddy ruffling my hair, "good night and you can sleep in tomorrow, today was a big day for all of us."

The next morning I wake up before nine and when I don't hear anyone moving around, I stay in bed and grab my laptop out of my backpack. The light in my room comes from a crack in the curtains, it looks grey outside. A good reason to stay here.

Opening the laptop, the screen is as bright as headlights in my darkened room. I reduce the glare and type in the A-Alliance website, I want to know more about when I'll have all my magic.

But I need a password to get into the site. "Arrgh!" I yell and slam the laptop shut. I decide to go downstairs and see what's for breakfast.

As I reach the kitchen I transform. "Mummy, Daddy?" I meow but I'm on my own. I have no idea where they are. I want to go outside, they may be out in the backyard, but the backdoor is closed. I prance over to the door and meow as loud as I can while scratching at the door. Then it opens.

"Logan, look at you. You're bigger than the last time." This is mummy talking as she picks me up giving me a cuddle. I purr and rub my head against her chin.

Daddy smiles at me, "Nice to see you again, Logan the

Kitten. Obviously being around the Jacarandas yesterday has brought this on."

That was one of the first lessons I learned, how we have the power to transform. Jacaranda trees have magical sap and the purple flowers contain this sap. When we are around Jacarandas in full bloom our powers grow in strength. Glenndale, the suburb we live in, is like a sea of purple during October and November every year. We have one at the back of our yard too.

"Mummy, I want to go outside. Over to the Jacaranda," I meow.

"Of course, darling. But Logan, be careful climbing it, you haven't done that as a cat yet."

"I'm a cat, don't I have nine lives?" I purr as I head outside. The day is still grey and I can smell rain coming.

I reach the tree and with three pounces I'm on one of the top branches. The tree is beginning to lose its flowers as it's near the end of the season. I peer over the top of houses and can just see the ocean, our home is not as close to the beach as the one Daddy grew up in.

With the tree being almost bare, my power isn't being strengthened, but it feels good being up here and knowing I can always count on the tree being in full bloom during October and November.

CHAPTER 5

LOGAN

A Kitten meets A Dog

We're all at assembly for the beginning of Term 4. It's October and warmth is in the air, we can't wait to start going to the beach again. Daddy has said I can learn to surf and join Nippers, the junior surf lifesaving activity. Boy, am I looking forward to that.

Chloe is standing in front of me but she isn't talking to me right now. We had a fight about the fact she hasn't been given her magical power yet and I said she may not have one. "Yes I have," she huffed, "my magical teacher told me. What makes you know everything," she had yelled at me.

At lunch, we're under the Jacaranda, Chloe is sitting next to Als and moves to the edge of the bench so I can't sit next to her. So, in spite, I sit opposite her.

"You can't ignore me for always. Look, I'm sorry, I was trying to be funny, but now know I was being mean."

"What's all this about?" asks Als.

"Nothing, we had a fight yesterday. Thanks, Logan, I like that you are sorry." Chloe says this with an unconvincing growl.

"And? What was the fight about?" Als continues much to my annoyance.

"It's nothing, Als ..." Before I can finish, there is this Ragdoll kitten, a ball of white fluff with brown tipped ears and paws, sitting next to Als. Luckily, Als was looking at me when this happened.

"Oh wow, where did you come from?" Als picks up the kitten then looks around. "Where's Chloe gone?"

I pretend not to know and shrug my shoulders while watching Als cuddling Chloe the Ragdoll telling it how gorgeous it is. "We had better get you somewhere safe."

"Um, here, give it to me. I'll take it to the office, they'll find the owner, I'm sure." Without waiting for Als to say anything, I grab Chloe the Ragdoll and make like I'm going to the office. When we're out of sight, Chloe jumps out of my hands.

"Huh, I proved you wrong. I do have magical powers," she meows.

"Well, one power for now. I'm happy for you. Now you had better stay out of sight until you transform back, you won't be a ragdoll for long." As I'm saying this the bell goes for us to return to class.

"You get to class, I'll go to mine when I transform. I'll tell my teacher I wasn't feeling well."

"Ok, good idea. And later we'll need to field questions from Als." This is something I'm not looking forward to.

Once I'm settled in class, our teacher introduces a boy who has started at our school today. His name is Jack Sterling and he has been buddied up with me. Taking a seat in front of me, we nod at each other. I don't know him, but his last name ... I think I know it. Why is that? Maybe my daddy has mentioned it.

At lunch, we're sitting under the Jacaranda as usual with Als having grilled us about the Ragdoll cat. We were saved from answering when Jack joined us. I introduce him to Chloe and Als.

"Hi, so where was your last school?" asks Als.

"We lived in Brisbane. My dad wanted to come back to his old home, and he told me there is more work for him here."

I look at him and ask about his father, "Umm, what is his name?"

"My dad? Noel. Why?"

Well that doesn't mean anything, my daddy hasn't mentioned knowing a Noel. "Nothing, your last name is ... oh, don't worry, it's not important. So, what do you like to do, Jack?" I want to talk about something different.

Jack tells us he enjoys listening to music and really likes musical theatre. I don't know anything about musical theatre but I like the way he is talking about it, his face is happy as he speaks and he is almost singing telling us how much he enjoys it. Both Chloe and Als seem to like him and I like him too, I think we're going to be friends.

It's only a few days later that Chloe and I learn Jack is a magical. He transformed into a Jack Russel as we were walking home. We were surprised when he hid behind a tree. When we checked what was happening there was a cute little Jack Russel looking up at us with dark-rimmed, puppy-dog eyes.

"Oh, Jack, look at you. You're one of us," coos Chloe.

This made the three of us best friends.

I'm watching TV in our lounge room when daddy walks in. "Hey buddy, how was your day at school today?" He sits on the sofa next to me. He's barefoot because he leaves his work boots outside and he's rubbing his feet. "Oh, my feet hurt. I stood up all day."

"Daddy, do you know someone called Noel? I met a boy today, Jack, he's new at our school. His last name, ahh what was it? Can't remember, but do you?"

He turns to look at me while still rubbing his feet. How do feet get sore? Mine don't hurt. "That's nice, you made a new friend. I did know someone called Noel, but we didn't call him by that name. He wasn't a nice person. Is that your new friend's father?"

My brain won't let me remember the name and I'm getting mad with myself. "Ah, yeah." Then I remember, "That's it, Jack Sterling. His daddy is Noel Sterling."

Daddy's face changes to a funny look, is he angry? I'm not sure but he stands up and says, "I'm glad you made a new friend, Logan. Now, I need a shower."

I watch him walking away wondering why Daddy is upset. Or maybe he isn't? I don't know how adults think.

School moves along quickly and before we know it, we're in Year 6. Me, Jack and Chloe. Jack now has a brother at our school too, Matthew, who everyone calls Matt. He's not as nice as Jack, in fact, I don't like him at all. The way he treats Jack you would think he's the older brother.

Als has already moved onto high school. The Fabulous Four as my parents nicknamed us, were separated. We're all going to join her in the next couple of years. She says she can't wait because she misses seeing us every day.

Everyone is proud of me because I'm school captain. My daddy is especially proud, he hugged me in a bear-like hug when I told him. Mum was pleased too, she didn't stop kissing me. Chloe and Jack are so buzzed about being the friends of the school captain, and do I feel awesome about that. Sure, there are responsibilities with being captain, but I have no problem because I can handle stuff. I've handled the bullies haven't I?

Let me explain. In Year 1 when Jack and I met, Jack was sensitive and what the girls called, *'a lit boy'*. This means he was popular and cute. Alex and Callum, the bullies at our school, picked up on Jack's sensitivity. They gave Jack hell. At one point, they pushed him off his bike because he wouldn't give them what they wanted and he ended up with a broken ankle. His parents had a lot to say about that and the bullies were given detention for weeks. The fact that these bullies targeted a kid like Jack, who is small for his age and wouldn't ever hurt anyone, gave us the urge to fight back.

That's exactly what we did. What the bullies didn't know is that we had power over them.

Jack, Chloe and I can all transform. Me into a Maine Coon cat, Jack into a Jack Russel, and Chloe into a Ragdoll. As we grew, we began transforming more often and by Year 6, were able to control when we did transform. Well, most of the time.

We were able to use our animal forms to annoy, no that's not quite right ... to scare the crap out of Alex and Callum to the point we were always in stitches after each attack. Jack especially enjoyed himself as the yappy Jack Russell who would attack their ankles and rip their school trousers to shreds. Chloe, as the irresistible ragdoll, was able to lure the two bullies into an area where Jack and I were waiting for them. When this didn't work because they realised it was a trap, we were ready for them anyway. It was a relief when these two bullies left to go to high school.

The three of us became a feature around school as our animal forms, although everyone did wonder where the hell we came from and who owned us when we suddenly appeared. We were a menace to the bullies but adorable to everyone else.

As I was school captain this did deter Alex and Callum a bit because I was with teachers more and generally doing my duties. This gave me confidence, something I was going to need when I started high school.

CHAPTER 6

Edward
　　The A-Alliance Committee

I've been part of the committee for years now, the A-Alliance voted me in after bestowing me with an achievement award. Part of my duties are to help Ester and the other seven committee members with the financials, the magical rules, and keeping our secret safe. Non-magicals must never find out about us magicals, they would not understand. I have heard people talk about wizards and witches in awful terms over the years. But that is the least of my worries.

Recently, there have been rumours of a group of magicals who want me gone from the A-Alliance. Ester has called me to the house to discuss the latest mistruths and fake news she has heard.

As I wait for her to finish making us tea, my nerves reach a height as tall as the jacaranda growing in this house. I breathe. Exhaling heavily.

"Calm down, Edward. We can fix this. You'll see." Ester says this as she places the hot tea in front of me. It's black like my mood.

"I'm not so sure Ester, the rumours are escalating."

"They are. Henry and Garrett are pushing others to follow their lead. They have added Wade, Kinley-Lee and Vera to their off-shoot group already."

"Great. Now there are five. It was bad enough with two of them hassling me with sneers and heckles. How do I compete with Henry and Garrett? Their lineage goes back centuries."

Ester sighs. Placing her cup down with minute precision, she looks me straight in the eye, "If you start thinking like that, you will lose. Yes, their families have had an influence with the Alliance, but it doesn't mean that these two bumblers are in that league."

Despite my mood, I laugh. She is right, Henry and Garrett are not known for their intelligence. However, the other three ... well they are whole other story. *The Five* is a force I'd rather not have to deal with. That's what I'll call them from now on, The Five. It wasn't enough I had to deal with bullies at school, now, as an adult, I have another nemesis for me to worry about.

Ester continues to fill me in on what she has heard. Wade has taken over from the two bumblers, which causes a bigger problem. Wade's father was second-in-charge to Garrett's grandfather, Alfred. He ran the A-Alliance committee for 100 years. He was a force and worse still, he was revered. Kinley-Lee and Vera are distantly related with their lineage also dating back centuries. "Granted, Edward, we have to deal with this situation with caution but it is not insurmountable."

"Forgive me for not agreeing, Ester. I inherited my

magic from Milly, I wasn't born into this world like all of you. If five magicals go against me, it will be an uphill battle for me to remain in the committee." I shudder as I remember the five of them, on separate occasions, giving me evil looks at the past few meetings. My nerves are on edge, I gulp the remaining tea pushing down my fear.

"Right. And how many of the five have achieved what you have despite being born into this society we call magicals? In fact, how many of us have had rules changed for the non-magicals to the point it has benefited them throughout their school years?"

Ester is correct. The *No Tolerance Bullying* rules were implemented in all schools after I, as Milly the Cat, fought bullies and with Trudi's help, gathered all the nerds into a group to counter bullies. "Sure, but I didn't do it on my own. I had help from the group."

She lets out a frustrated gasp. "Edward, you must stop being so negative. With this attitude you may as well give up now." She stands and takes both cups to the sink. Turning to me with both hands behind her back holding onto the sink, she continues, "Listen, you achieved a great deal in a short amount of time, use this knowledge to fight this fight. There are more in the Alliance who are on your side, those five cannot compete with the might of the whole magical society."

I stand and move towards Ester. In a rare show of emotion towards her, I give her a hug. She pats my back with one hand, slow and steady. She knows I've got this.

Back home Sally is waiting for me. Her eyes are wide with questions. I sit at the dining table and she follows suit. "We're going to formulate a plan." I continue explaining who the five are.

"Wade. He spells trouble. Henry and Garrett we could have handled, but now...

"I know, Sally. I'm worried too. Actually, I'm scared, more now than ever. What was I thinking accepting this honour from the Alliance? There are many more magicals who should be in my place."

She places her hand on my knee, "From what you've told me, this is exactly how they want you to think. Ester is right, you have achieved more in the years since Milly passed than many magicals achieve in a lifetime."

My love for her soars and swells as I move towards her and kiss her with fervour. She gives me the strength I am going to need to fight these bullies at the A-Alliance.

CHAPTER 7

LOGAN

High School and The Five

We're in the quadrangle looking around, the February heat searing our feet through our school shoes. The asphalt is like molten lava.

Most of us have parents who attended here, our surnames are known. This makes us targets for the other bullies at this school. Alex and Callum are not the only ones we have to worry about.

Als comes over to greet us. "Hey, it's great to have you with me every day again. And next year, Chloe will join us. Welcome to Redman High. Looking forward to your party this weekend, Logan."

"Yeah, thanks," I reply while Jack smiles back at her. It's my 13th birthday she is referring to. "How are things here? I've heard Alex and Callum have already made friends with the other bullies."

"It's a problem, I guess. They've left me alone, but now

you are both here, who knows what they will do. But I'm glad you're here. Missed you guys." Her arms spread indicating a group hug, which we fall into. I've missed seeing her every day too.

Sunshine floods our backyard as everyone mingles about. My party is in full swing and I love the fact everyone invited has turned up. My family, my friends ... and no bullies in sight. I can relax and enjoy my birthday.

Jack comes up behind me as I'm staring towards the Jacaranda. "Hey, what's going on? Shouldn't you be mingling with all of us?"

"Uh, oh sure. Just catching my breath."

"Will you stop worrying, Alex and his crew won't crash this party. Not if they know what's good for them. We are both able to control our magic and can take them on." Jack says this with a flourish of his hand, indicating he dismisses them as a problem.

"I know, Jack, but I don't want anything spoiling this party. Anyway, you're right, I should not be worrying about those idiots. Come on, it's time I cut my cake."

I'm standing behind my cake with Mum and Dad. I place the knife down after cutting my cake and now everyone wants photos. It's like paparazzi city, there are so many phones we don't know which one to look at first. That's when I hear his voice. "Where you at, pretty boy?" It's Alex and he's not looking for me, he's after Jack. Pretty Boy is the nickname the bullies have bestowed on Jack.

My dad looks at me, concern seeping over his face. "What the hell is he doing here?"

"It's fine, Dad, Jack and I will handle this. Please don't make it worse by getting involved." I move away from the cake table and head towards Alex and Callum. Jack is already standing at the top of our driveway telling them not to go any further.

Alex looks over Jack's shoulder to see me coming and continues the verbal abuse, "Oh, your boyfriend has come for backup." He sneers at me while Callum has a dopey look on his face. "Hey, Jack, where's that smart brother of yours?"

Matt was back with the rest of my friends, although technically he's not my friend. I had to invite him because he's Jack's little brother, he's an annoying little shit even though he's taller than Jack. Matt rubs me up the wrong way when he blabs about things like he knows everything, he's more of a show-off and an attention-seeker than his older brother.

"You two had better leave, there is nothing for you to see here," Jack commands them with his hands on his hips.

Both Alex and Callum laugh. Alex pumps out more garbage about being offended they were not invited. "You invite us and we leave you alone, didn't you know that?"

"Why should I invite you two? We're not friends. I'm waiting on the day you leave school, which won't be long now, you're both 16 now."

"We'll leave school when we're good and ready. Now, aren't you going to offer us some cake?"

"Alex, get going and take your idiot mate with you." Jack is brimming with authority, which makes me admire him more. He may be tiny, but he has attitude.

Before I can say anything, Dad and Uncle Jackson are behind us. "You heard Jack, it's time you ran along home. Or do I need to call the authorities?"

Alex and Callum sneer at Jack and I before walking back towards our front gate. Even though I had asked my dad not to become involved, I'm glad he did. And Uncle

Jackson with tats covering one arm, probably gave them a right fright. Jack may have acted brave, but I know we are no match for those two bullies in our human form.

The rest of the afternoon sees us enjoying games, music and me opening my presents. Apart from a brotherly spat between Jack and Matt, which is a common occurrence, nothing else ruined my party.

A couple of weeks later, I'm in the kitchen of the Alliance house getting drinks for us when I hear mumbling coming from the front room. Curious, I gingerly walk towards the door that is ajar, my heart thumping. I peek inside to see five members, three sitting on the lounge and two standing, one is talking. It's dim and I can't see who they are, but I do recognise Wade's voice. I overhear him mentioning my dad's name and then what they are planning. Horrified, I run back through the kitchen forgetting the drinks and rush to where the others are standing.

"Hey, have you seen my dad?" I ask Chloe and Jack who are playing with an alpaca and a llama.

"He's over there with Jack's mum and other adults. What's wrong, why are you puffing?"

"Nothing, I'll tell you later. Must speak with my dad first." I rush over to the food table where the adults are and whisper to Dad that he follow me. I head away from everyone before he can answer me.

I run towards a group of Jacarandas making sure no one else is around. Dad catches up with me and asks what the hell is going on.

"I heard Wade with others in the house, the front room ..." I stop as I catch my breath. It takes me a minute as I'm in the middle of a panic attack.

Dad places his hands on my shoulders knowing exactly

what to do, panic attacks are part of my life now and have been for a few years. "Ok, slow down. Breathe. Take your time and tell me everything." He knows I'm upset because this is usually what brings on these attacks.

My palms are clammy, my breathing is slowing down and I look at my father with tears edging towards my cheeks. "Wade and four others were in the front room talking about you. His voice was low but I could tell he was angry, his words were spat out. They want to get rid of you, why?"

Indicating we sit on the bench under one of the trees, Dad says, "They are unhappy about me being on the committee. They're jealous. But I don't want you to worry about it, Ester and I are keeping tabs on what they're doing." He places his arm over my shoulders bringing me in close, "Logan, they're upset that someone like me who inherited his magic can have such a position of power and I guess they have a point. Ester is summoning others for a meeting next week to discuss how to stop them. Please stay calm, we will sort this."

I look up at him with trusting eyes. He wipes away my tears then stands up, "Come on, let's go, I think it's time for one of Ester's wonderful milkshakes."

CHAPTER 8

LOGAN
The Sucker Punch

Year 8 and Chloe joins us at high school. It's great having the *Fabulous Four* back together. This is the latest name our parents bestowed on us. And the more people we have to keep the bullies at bay, the better.

Chloe, Jack, Als and I are sitting at the top of the oval under shade. Jack's brother Matt is sitting away from us, he and Jack had yet another fight. Over something stupid of course, Matt has a way of getting under Jack's skin and I get it, he's a knob.

It's after school and we're waiting for our parent's to pick us up. We're talking about what we're doing this weekend and I tell them I'm heading to the beach.

"Great, I'll see you there," says Jack. "Usual spot?"

"Yep, 11-ish I think. Girls, are you coming?" They both nod but don't talk, the heat sapping their energy. I'm about to say something else when we hear Alex yelling.

"Hey pretty boy, watcha doin' this weekend?"

"Ignore them, Jack. Your mum will be here any minute."

"I'm trying to, Logan." He says this as he jumps the fence and moves closer to the road. Matt languishes behind him oblivious to what is going on. He never helps or becomes involved, much to my anger. He really is a useless brother.

I stand up too with the girls following. By this time Alex and Callum have reached us.

"You chicken. Don't ya want to talk to us pretty boy."

"Lay off, Alex. You two have gone overboard this week."

"Logan, it's your fault. If you'd invited us to your party, we wouldn't be pissed with you all."

Frustration seeps into my body, "We're not friends. And why pick on Jack so much?" Alex had recently opened Jack's backpack throwing everything in it onto the ground. Luckily, Jack was holding his laptop. A few books were dog-eared and Jack's ego was bruised, yet again, but this was a lucky escape. The bullies have broken a few laptops recently.

"That freak is an easy target. And why are you always protecting him, is he your boyfriend now?"

Jack had come out before my birthday, not that this was such a secret. I admire his bravery and glad he owns who he is, but now he is targeted even more by all the bullies at this school.

Alex is heading towards the fence just as Jack's mother pulls up. Both Jack and Matt jump in the car. This is a lucky escape and I breathe a sigh of relief.

But things aren't over. Alex and Callum head towards me, the scowls on their faces unsettling. "Give me a break …

really! You're that upset about not being invited to my party?"

Alex booms expletives at me as I shield the girls from him. "We've had enough of your bullshit and the cats and that stupid dog you throw at us. Not being invited was the final straw." With that he clocks me right on the nose and I buckle at the knees.

The girls scream with Als throwing punches at Alex, "Look what you've done, you idiot." She bends down gathering her school shirt out of her skirt and using it against my nose to stop the bleeding.

My dad and aunt Trudi drive up when all this is happening. They jump out of their cars but Alex and Callum are shooting off down the oval and disappearing.

Dad is the first to ask what's happened. The teacher fills him in and my father sees red, he is angrier than I've ever seen him. "This is unacceptable. I will be reporting this to the police and speaking with the principal."

Half an hour later, I'm sitting in emergency, my nose sporting an ice pack. I'm drowsy and fed up. Dad is sitting next to me texting mum about what has happened. The fury is in his fingers as he attacks the keypad. He had asked the teacher to file a report into the incident and I'm sure he's telling mum everything he has put in place since turning up at school.

I want to lie down but was told to stay upright. I understand my father's frustration. I'm sure something will happen to those bullies this time, they have gone too far this time.

After a few days at home with my face resembling a squished, overripe blueberry, I'm bored. My eye sockets are purple, yellow and red, I can barely see.

And with my nose bandaged, it feels heavy and is blocked. I see stars every time I touch it. I'm feeling sorry for myself and can't believe I'm actually missing school. But I am using this time wisely because Jack, Chloe and I have been discussing how we're going to get our revenge. Alex is going down, he will regret ever messing with us.

Weeks later, the school bell rings as we head for our classrooms. My face is looking somewhat better, but everyone was fascinated by the bruising when I arrived at school. Jack said it was a privilege to be looking like this after saving him. How I saved him, I'm not sure, his ride arrived before Alex could get to him. Then I was targeted instead.

My lessons and classes are no different to when I had last been at school two weeks ago. And in this last week, I was able to see well enough to be doing my work at home. I haven't missed that much and I'm glad to be back, it's great being with my friends again.

I'm packing my bag after a double science lesson when the principal's assistant asks me to follow her, "The Principal wants to have a word," she says with a plum in her mouth. She's the only person I know who speaks English with this posh accent. I follow behind mimicking her and everyone left in the room snickers.

When I'm in the principal's office, he asks me to sit. "You're lucky things were not worse, young man. The other boy has been suspended and his cohorts have been reprimanded. We have zero tolerance to this kind of behaviour thanks to your father and his efforts when he was at this school. I'm glad to see you back, but a warning – try not to provoke these boys."

"Yes, Sir. But we were minding our own business waiting for our rides home. How is this provoking them?"

He shifts in his oversized chair, harrumphs and sits forward placing his arms on his desk. He looks me straight in the eyes, "I understand it takes almost nothing to provoke those boys, I'm asking you to be more aware. Possibly yell for help, there are always teachers around."

"Yes, Sir." This is all I say because he has no idea how bullies work, there is usually no time to call out for help. This may even lead to a bigger beating before teachers can arrive to save the day. "Is that all, Sir?"

"Yes young man, off you go. Give my regards to your father."

I nod then stand and leave his office. I head towards the school gate only to be confronted by Alex. I head in another direction to avoid him.

"Wait. I ... I didn't mean to hurt you, not this much. Your face looks ok tho'," he says kicking his feet on the grass.

"What? You're apologising."

"Well, yeah. I'm not a monster. I was tryin' to scare ya, that's all."

I'm surprised and don't really know what to say. "Umm, ok. Thanks. I guess." Perplexed, I walk heading to the other gate and hope he doesn't follow me. I wonder where his guilt trip has come from, or is it a ploy to catch me off guard?

When I'm home and in my room, I'm chatting with Jack and Chloe. Als had been on the chat too but had to go and do some chores. Now we can talk freely about Alex.

Jack writes –

Big deal, he semi-apologised, so what? We should still retaliate, it's time to bring back the animals, they've been dormant for a while. There is no way he should get away with this.

I write –

You should have seen his face, there was remorse there, I swear. Maybe we should let this go.

Chloe writes –

Wow, this is big. Maybe Alex has a heart after all.

Jack sends a laughing emoji.

I write –

Maybe he does, why else would he apologise?

Jack writes –

Because he wants to give you a false sense of security. I wouldn't trust him.

Chloe writes –

I agree. Don't trust him, Logan. It is time to bring our animals back. We've let him get away with too much. And as usual, Matt was useless. He doesn't stand up for you at all, Jack.

Jack writes –

My brother is a loser, he lives in his own little world. He annoys the hell out of me, we're always fighting. Our mum gets frustrated, dad thinks it's boys being boys. Me, I hate the little shit.

I write -

I've always wanted a brother or sister but seeing you two fight constantly has banished that thought. I'm happy the way things are, I have all of you, that's enough for me.

I hear my mum call me for dinner - Hey guys, gotta go, dinner's ready. See you tomorrow at school.

They both send waving hand emojis and I head down for dinner.

CHAPTER 9

Edward
  Old and New Foes

It's Saturday afternoon and we've had a family movie afternoon. Marvel movies are always good and this latest Thor didn't disappoint.

"That was cool," says Logan as we walk out of the theatre into the bright sunshine. His face has healed but his nose is slightly crooked, it bends more to the left now. He sneezes. This happens often too, it's a side effect of the punch he received from Alex. His panic attacks have also increased. To say Sally and I are upset about what happened is an understatement, but the school handled it well and Alex is still suspended. He's not allowed back at school until Term 2 and only if he completes the anti-bullying course and passes. Luckily for us, he and Callum will be leaving school next year, they are both in Year 11 now. I fully intend to keep a close eye on all the bullies now, there is no way I want another school student hurt like Logan was.

We walk a few steps when we hear Logan being called by Jack who is sitting with his parents at the café next to the movie theatre. I know they are his parents because Hannah is sitting with him, I've seen her at the A-Alliance with Jack a few times. The man sitting next to her is Buster, my old nemesis.

I'm not keen to see Buster again, but Mad Marion, a local homeless lady, was heading towards us. I was happy to avoid her as we head into the café.

Logan runs over to Jack, "Hi. Hey, just saw the Thor movie, what a blast. Have you seen it?" He and Jack are deep in conversation by the time Sally and I arrive at the café. Matt is being totally ignored but has his face in his phone anyway. Logan drags a chair over and sits down.

"Hello, Hannah."

"Hi, Edward, hello Sally. You both know my husband, Noel, right?"

"Edward, good to see you." Buster puts his hand out, which I ignore.

"Buster." I remain as calm as I can even though I need all my strength not to pummel his face. After all these years, I still hate this guy. Also, even though I knew he and Hannah were married, I didn't feel any animosity towards her. Maybe because she is actually nice and a healing magical. She has the power to heal some illnesses with the power of her mind and touch. Something I've witnessed a few times when magical kids have had mishaps.

"Hmm, cool, I get you're still pissed, Edward. I moved on a long time ago, what do you say we leave the past back where it should be?"

I hate the fact he has a point and with Sally now sitting

next to Hannah also deep in conversation, I have no choice but to talk to Buster. "You bullied me for years, it's not an easy thing to get over. Besides, seeing you now has brought it all back." How do I forget all the torment? He is not someone I want to be friends with. I dismiss all those bad memories for now.

He indicates I sit, but I tell him I'm fine standing. I don't want to be here any longer than we need to be. Mad Marion has moved away taking her smell with her. There is no need for us to stay and avoid her now.

"Come on, you guys gave back as much as we gave you. That bloody pet cat you had was brutal."

"Not mine actually. Don't you remember the old lady down my street looked after it."

"Whatever, it was always around and those scratches festered. I can't stand cats now."

I admit having Milly the Cat around did help our cause. Trudi and Jackson are still the only non-magicals who know I can transform. They know the three of us are magicals and keep our secret safe. They also love the fact their daughter, Chloe, is magical. Jackson had a great uncle who was a magical. This is how some non-magical parents end up with a magical child, it is a throw-back from a few generations.

"Come on, Edward. Let's forget about what happened years ago. I've changed, I have my two boys and a beautiful wife, I'm no longer that person."

Sally looks up at me, "It was a long time ago, honey. Logan and Jack are friends, it's time to let the past go."

I'm not sure I trust Buster, who now wants to be called Noel, but I am trapped and decide to be civil. "Noel, it's nice to see you again," I say offering him my hand. We shake.

We spend the next half an hour, sipping coffees and

talking about what they have been up to. They moved back to Glenndale after Noel's mother passed away, his stepfather had left her soon after Noel had left home. "I couldn't wait to get out of this shithole, but now I'm older, I can see the value in the place. We've renovated the old dump into a comfortable home and the boys enjoy living close to the beach. I do odd jobs for people now, I'm a bit of a handyman, so if you need help Edward, I'll give you a good deal."

And there is the old, cocky Buster. He's going to give me a *good deal*. I scoff at him, "Gee thanks, Noel, I'll keep that in mind. Well, this has been great, but it's time we leave you guys to it. Come on Logan, Sally."

"Oh, Dad, we're still talking."

"You can keep chatting at home online, I have work to do."

"On a Saturday?" Logan whines and I am annoyed because he knows I do paperwork on Saturdays.

I don't answer because all I want to do is get away from Noel before he offers me something else I don't want to hear about.

Ester has organised a special meeting at the A-Alliance house to discuss the uprising of *The Five*. This group has upped their game in trying to get me dispelled from the Alliance by pushing their cause with other members. They are unnerving me every time we cross paths with Wade *accidentally* bumping into me and sneering as he walks past. *"So, sorry Edward, didn't see you there."* This was his paltry excuse.

The Committee is seated at the head table in the courtroom, Ester managed to summon many of the other members to listen to what she has to say. The committee members are already on my side. Looking around the dim courtroom, I notice Hannah seated near the front. She smiles mouthing, "You've got this."

"Thank you all for coming, we all appreciate you making the effort to attend this extraordinary meeting. As you all know, The Five – Henry, Garrett, Wade, Kinley-Lee and Vera, are all wanting to remove Edward from the committee. In fact, not only from the committee, but also ban him from the Alliance altogether." She waits while the murmurs and whispers die down before continuing. "They are jealous of Edward's rise and I know you have all been approached by them, so the fact you are all here gives me hope. Edward is not going anywhere as far as I'm concerned." The loudness of the cheers and claps puts a wide smile on Ester's face. She sits and gives me the floor.

I clear my throat, "Good evening to you all. Same as Ester, I appreciate you all being here. As far as we know, The Five has not approached any magicals overseas, but this doesn't mean it hasn't happened. We need to move fast to stop them." Continuing, I tell them of the ideas the committee has come up with and ask for any feedback and other ideas they may have. "I understand I am only one member of the committee and was not born a magical, but I feel at home at this Alliance, I consider you all friends and our goal of keeping this magical group secret is my priority. I know I have more to give." Once the clapping has subsided, I give them more reasons why I should be kept on and hope I'm doing enough for them to agree to help. Once I finish my speech, my voice raspy and my mouth parched from talking, we break up and move outside to the meadow, where the food and drinks are set up for us.

. . .

"The Five is going about this all wrong."

I recognise her voice. Hannah is behind me, I turn around and say hello. "What do you mean?"

"They are showing their hatred of you to the point the other members are already fed up. Don't forget you're liked more than they are."

"Thanks Hannah, I appreciate you saying that. But the fact remains, they are a menace we have to deal with."

"Agreed, but you have the numbers behind you, take heart in that. Oh, by the way, are you and Noel good? I noticed you were tense the other day when we talked."

I had been thinking how we had met after the movie at the café and have tried to think about liking that man, but I admit it's not easy. I could do without Noel and Matt, I've seen how Matt treats Jack and it reminds me of the bullying tactics of his father. I don't trust either of them. Hannah, on the other hand, along with Jack, is fine. I look over Hannah's head in case others are listening, "Yes, of course, it's all in the past. By the way, where does he think you are tonight? It's only a couple of weeks since our last meeting."

"Oh, so you know he has no idea about Jack and I being magicals?" I nod, Sally had told me and I let Hannah know this. "Right, I had told Sally. Well, I have a group of female friends who regularly meet for dinner, he thinks I'm with them."

"Oh ok. Do you think he suspects something? He did see me transform once."

"I don't think so. He doesn't talk about his past much so I didn't know this. How did you explain what happened?"

"It's a long story for another time." I don't want to go into how we used the altering memory magic on Noel. "Now, I'm sorry, I have to mingle, thanks for your support, Hannah."

"I'm here if you need me." I nod telling her I appreciate her support. Then I move towards other committee members, I need to not think about Noel right now. The bullies in my current life are worse than Noel ever was and I'm not sure who I can trust at the A-Alliance anymore.

CHAPTER 10

The Geeks

Alex returned to school without learning his lesson. Although he isn't physical for now, he still expects geeks to give him lunch money, by taunting them and putting them down with his harsh words. And his group of bullies has grown. Alex and Callum now have Donovan and Parker. Occasionally, Donovan's girlfriend, Miller, and Parker's girl-friend, Scarlett, become involved. This has been going on for months.

After handing over my money yet again, I am pissed. I walk over to where the others are with a plan formulating in my mind. "Right, I've had enough. We need to do some-thing now before Alex's power grows stronger."

"We're listening," says Jack.

"I've spoken to Tahlia, Manuel, Aaron and Georgia. They're all fed up too."

"So much for Alex passing his bullying course. He's

been worse since coming back to school. He's even targeting people online again. Wasn't he banned from contacting us online?"

"He was, Jack, but who is going to stop him? But, with the help of the other four geeks, we can reduce his power and give him an incentive to stop cyber bullying. We can form a group similar to what my father organised, each of us can recruit geeks to join us. The more people we have, the better. I'm not giving up any more of my money and I don't want to hear of others feeling less than they are."

Chloe stands up as the school bell rings, "Great, I'll send out messages, you guys do the same. There will be safety in numbers. See you all after school."

"Perfect. We can all meet this Friday to work out how this will work."

Twenty of us have gathered at a park, one that happens to be opposite the A-Alliance house. Maybe this is a good omen. It's the last day of term so I thank everyone for coming. "I know you've all had enough with the bullies, but with only one term left this year, Alex, Callum and a few of the others will only be at school for another year. We can do some serious damage and teach them once and for all we mean business. It's time they left us alone." Everyone cheers and claps filling the park with this positive noise.

"This is long overdue, you four have handled them well enough, but with our help, you're right Logan, we will teach them a lesson."

"Thanks Manuel, we appreciate your support mate. Look, rather than reinvent the wheel, we can use a tactic my father used, film the bullies attacking us and threaten to post. By threatening to expose them, we can take away their power. We'll use Alex's cyber bullying against him. Let him see how it feels."

"Sounds good," says Aaron, "And at other times we can all gang up on them, twenty of us is a force, don't you think? We can change things."

I agree with Aaron and we continue discussing how and when to deploy these ideas until the late afternoon. We eventually split up and head our separate ways wishing each other a great holiday and looking forward to a better Term 4.

Only Jack and I are left at the park. His head is down, he looks despondent. "What's going on?"

"Nothing, another fight with Matt, that's all. He wants to join this group, which is weird because he doesn't seem that interested. He isn't targeted by the bullies, why would he want to be a part of this?"

We start walking home as I answer. "We always need more recruits and maybe his weird personality, you know, fighting for no reason and generally hating you, might fuel him to help fight the bullies instead of you?"

He ponders this for a moment, "Maybe."

"Look, let him join, it can't hurt. He's stocky and has an angry resting face, I think he might be useful."

Jack looks at me and nods. It's not an enthusiastic nod, but I'm going to allow Matt to join us. We can always boot him out if he becomes a menace.

It doesn't take long before us geeks have to implement our ideas. A week into Term 4 and Alex has bullied money out of both Jack and Manuel. We're there with our cameras on both occasions.

At the first bullying of Jack, they think we're bluffing.

"This is bullshit, you're not going to post anything." Alex spits these word at us. When we all show our phones with tweets and posts ready to go, Jack is given back some of his money. Alex and Callum had already spent some of it.

The second time with Manuel, they hadn't learned their lesson yet again. Alex and Callum grab Manuel by the shirt collar demanding he hand over money. This time the geek group was ready and threatened to call the teachers if they didn't leave Manuel alone. We also had our phones ready.

"You are all full of shit," says Alex removing his hands from Manuel's shirt. "Come on boys, I've had enough of these geeks."

They move away from us as we all smile and congratulate each other. I know Alex can't risk being caught by a teacher and risking more than just a suspension, he will be expelled the next time teachers find him bullying someone. This is something else we have over him.

Donovan and Miller along with Parker and Scarlett, the other bullies in Alex' group, follow him and glare back at us, particularly at me. I shiver wondering if we've gone too far, Donovan and Parker, who are a year younger than Alex and Callum, have two more years at this school. I mention this to the others, "We had better keep an eye of those four too, they're going to give us trouble."

Both Manuel and Aaron agree with Manuel adding, "They've gone under the radar while Alex has been doing everything, but you're right Logan, they are just biding their time.

Year 12 comes and goes for Alex and Callum. We manage to keep them at bay but we have had to rely on our animals a few times. Jack was particularly great when he and Chloe stopped three Year 7 kids being bullied. Chloe as the Ragdoll Cat ran through the bullies legs putting them off balance, and then Jack as the yappy Jack Russel was nipping at Alex and Callum's ankles. We were all in stitches watching them trying to catch Jack, but he was too nimble and fast. Both Chloe and Jack were chased towards the back oval while the Year 7 kids watched in awe at what just happened. The relief on their faces was priceless.

Alex and Callum tapered off with their bullying. Maybe we did change their thinking by all of us geeks taking them on? Matt had also helped a few times by talking them down. Jack and I were pleased to see that Matt actually came through for us. He was part geek after all.

But we found out at the end of the school year why the bullies really gave up, both of them were warned by teachers if they caused more problems they would not be graduating. In the end, the teachers helped our cause too.

However, we were right about the other bullies. Donovan and Parker upped their game, especially with the younger Year 7 kids. They were physical and intimidating, both of them stocky with faces that challenged and scared those younger than them. They didn't stop at just the boys either, girls were targeted too. We overheard them telling their girlfriends that girls were easier targets, they gave their money over straight away. Sometimes they didn't have to say anything, their scowling faces scared the hell out of the girls. Poor things.

We did our best to stop them, but Donovan and Parker were sneakier than Alex and Callum, they were more street smart and picked the right time to bully. Usually, they picked on kids in the early morning and after school. We also heard reports of them bullying kids at the shops when they're parents weren't around. Then, of course, there was the cyber bullying.

On the last day of school, us geeks met to discuss how to deal with these two. We came up with a plan to put in place once we were back at school next year, those two are not going to beat us.

CHAPTER 11

Edward

Leaving the Past Behind

I arrive home from work glad it's a Friday. I know I still have paperwork to do this weekend, but it's a break from the physical work I do all week.

Sally and Logan are in the kitchen preparing dinner. Logan says, "Hey Dad, we're having hamburgers, you hungry?"

I kiss Sally hello and reply, "For hamburgers, definitely. I'll go and freshen up."

When I come back into the kitchen, the sweet smell of fried onions teases my nose making me even hungrier. "Ok, what can I do to help?"

"No, we've got this. You sit, they're basically ready," says Sally.

I'm happy to hear this and sit at the table ready to devour a burger. I've been so stressed about The Five I haven't eaten much since the extraordinary meeting. It's great to be sitting in my home with the two people I love the most in the world and forgetting about my problems for a night.

Later, once Logan has gone to bed, we're sitting on the lounge with our drinks. The television is on but we're talking, so basically ignoring it. "Seeing Buster ... I mean Noel, again was a bit of a shock. I can't believe we haven't run into him in all this time. Then again, it's rare that I'm at the mall on a Saturday afternoon, that's usually when I'm doing paperwork." That particular day I had decided to spend time with my family. And the movie was a good distraction.

"He really had an effect on you, didn't he?"

"I was bullied in primary school by others and Noel upped the ante at high school. Ha, I find it hard to call him that. Anyway, forming the group with Trudi and with the other geeks as well as having Milly the Cat around, helped me to cope. You know the rest of the story, it's got me to where I am today."

"That's what you need to focus on, look where you are. You have a successful building business, you're on the A-Alliance committee, and you have me. And Logan."

I move closer to her and kiss her. Her lips taste of the red wine we're drinking. "Thanks, it helps to hear that. But it's going to be hard for me to be friends with Noel."

"You like Hannah and Jack. Logan and Jack are friends. Noel doesn't know about them being magicals, so the chances of you running into him are slim. Look at how long it took for you to run into him, they moved back years ago."

She's right and I tell her so. But the niggling thought that I will run into Noel more now means I have to consider him as a friend. Or if not a friend, an acquaintance at least. I decide it might be easier to leave the past behind.

Logan comes running into the lounge, puffed and red-faced. "You're not going to believe ..." He takes a breath, "what Hannah did today."

Both Sally and I look at him wondering where he's been, it's after five. "Well, hello to you too," says Sally standing and placing her hands on her hips, "where have you been? I was about to call you."

"Yes, umm, sorry Mum. I was caught up. It's what I was about to tell you." Logan takes a seat, breathing a little easier. He wipes his arm on his sweaty brow. Sally heads to the kitchen to grab water for him.

"You know to let one of us know if you're going to be late." I look at him with concern feeling better now he is home.

Logan takes the drink from Sally and gulps it down. "Dad, Mum, I'm sorry but there wasn't time to ring or text, it all happened so fast." Sally and I sit down again and listen. "You know about Mad Marion, the homeless lady who walks our streets filthy and stinky with unwashed hair? We both nod. "Well, she was hanging around the school this afternoon and was being asked to leave by teachers. When she refused, the principal was called and that's when she went absolutely ballistic – swearing, throwing her arms about, shouting, *"I can stay here, it's a public space."* She spat this out making everyone move back in disgust. The police were called."

"Oh the poor thing, technically she wasn't doing anything wrong. I feel so sorry for her."

"It is sad, Sally. She was abused by her alcoholic father

from a young age and left abandoned at eight years old by both parents."

"We all know her story, Dad, but it doesn't change the fact no one wants her around. All of us give her a lot of space whenever she walks towards us, we usually cross the road or head the other way."

"Which makes it even worse for her. Imagine how she feels with everyone hating her."

"Do we have a choice, Mum? She's rabid, who knows what we can catch from her?"

Sally sighs, "This is the problem, no one wants to go near her so how is she meant to get any help?"

"The fact she is still alive amazes me," I say, "how awful to be living like that, no future in sight."

"Anyway, can I finish telling you what Hannah did?" We both nod again, apologetic looks on our faces. "Other students had all gone, there were only two teachers, the principal and Jack and I left. We were waiting for Hannah who arrived in time to see Marion's melt down. She helped the teachers in calming her down, her soft voice soothing. I'm sure she was using her healing powers because Marion stopped wailing immediately. The principal offered to call someone who could help her, a social worker maybe. Marion looked down to the pavement and muttered she didn't know anyone."

"Hannah then offered to take her to a community outreach centre, but only if she agreed to wash up and make herself more presentable. To our astonishment, Mad Marion nodded and followed Hannah to the girls toilets. When they returned, the gunk on her face was gone, her hair was tamed, and her hands were clean. Her nails needed more work, but that was a job for later."

Logan continues as we're both still interested in what

happened next. "Hannah places a towel on the back seat of the car and asks Marion to sit, which she does without complaint. Then Hannah tells the teachers and principal she will take Marion to the Glenndale Outreach Centre. They thank her and after I sit in the front seat, Jack opts to walk home. Not that I blamed him, Marion still smelt like rotting food scraps. But I felt bad if I had followed Jack, so I remained in the car,"

"Oh, how horrible for her. I'm sure the outreach centre was able to help. And good for you on staying put, I'm proud of you."

I look at mum smiling, "The Centre helped to a point, but I think it was Hannah's healing powers that helped more. When we arrived at the centre, a social worker was appointed to help Marion, giving her some clean clothes and showing her to the showers. Hannah placed her hand on Marion's arm and coaxed her to the bathroom section while I waited in reception. I was relieved not to be smelling that rotten smell coming from her."

"It was about a half hour later when they both emerged with Marion dressed, hair dripping but clean, and smelling a bit better. Hannah spoke to the social worker who said she would work out a plan for Marion and that she would get the help needed." I stop talking exhausted and hungry. "What's for dinner? I'm starving."

"Well, I'm happy to see this ordeal hasn't affected you. It's pasta tonight."

"Thanks Mum, I'll have a double helping. I'm going to shower now, that smell is still hanging around me."

We both watch as he walks away. It was a big ordeal he went through today, but it was good for him to see how Hannah's compassion and healing powers worked to subdue the poor homeless woman. "I'm proud of him, he stayed in the car when he had the chance to walk home with Jack."

"Me too, he chose to stay and help Hannah. What a lovely son we have." Pleased with ourselves, we head to the kitchen to prepare dinner.

I'm at work on a building site in the city. The meeting with the architect and engineer has finished and I place my hard hat back on, I have to oversee the pouring of the concrete. I'm heading to the scaffolding when I hear my name. I turn to see Noel near the front gate.

"Edward, I have a proposal for you. Do you have a minute?"

I don't but I allow him in anyway. "Look, I have to watch the concrete pour, talk to me while we walk over there. Here, put this on." He places my spare hard hat on. I'm not interested in working with Noel, but I can at least hear what he has to say.

"I have two others who I work with, one is a carpenter, the other an electrician. The three of us would like to offer you our services. At mates rates."

"Ok. Send me a proposal in writing and we can go from there. No promises though, I already have a good team."

"Sure, will do. I know you will like what we're proposing and you will save money, that is a promise."

"Ah, thanks. Now, you know the way out, right?"

His face shows his displeasure at being dismissed so quickly. "Ah, yeah, sure. I'll email you." He hands me back the hard hat.

I watch as he leaves and waves towards me after walking out of the gate. The idea of working with him is surreal and I'm going to have to forgive him for all the shit he put me through. Somehow I can't see this working.

When I arrive home, I head straight to my office and check emails. Noel's proposal is there. He was right about me saving money if I use their services, but me trusting Noel is an issue. I need to discuss this will Sally before I make any decisions.

Walking out to the backyard where Sally is putting out laundry, she smiles as I walk up to her. She looks pretty in her floral summer dress and still takes my breath away. I tell her about Noel coming to see me.

"He wants to work with you? You already have a good team. I'm not sure I like this idea."

"Well, the cost savings are significant, maybe I can give him a few projects, smaller ones." Although even the thought of doing this doesn't feel right,

"Working with friends is fraught with problems, ask my father about it. He lost a good friend by helping him out. And I lost a good friend too, his daughter. We were close for years."

I help her carry the laundry basket back inside, leaving it on the laundry bench. Following her into our kitchen, I say, "Technically, he's not my friend. And I would make sure the contract was iron-clad. The savings may be worth it."

"Hmm, being competitive is always good, but I have a bad feeling about this. I don't want to lose another friend, Hannah and I get on well. And what about Logan and Jack?"

Looking down at my feet, I realise I hadn't thought this through, it affected more people than just me. And do I really want another bully in my life? Even though Noel said he's no longer a bully, can I trust him? Also, I have The Five to deal with.

I decide not to give Noel any work, he can find work elsewhere because I'd rather keep my distance from him as much as possible. Sometimes you have to hedge your bets and even though his proposal was a good one, this is the right decision for all of us.

CHAPTER 12

Ailsa
  Jack's Secret

It's my last year at school and the thought of leaving makes me sad that I won't see my friends every day. Logan, Jack and Chloe will still be in high school, whereas I am finishing high school and contemplating going to university. I'm thinking of doing social work something my friends know I will be good at.

These summer school holidays are the best, we spend a lot of fun times together. It's all because Jack's father put in a pool. We spent many weekends at his place and the only bad thing was Matt, Jack's annoying little brother. We ignored him and he mostly had his nose in his phone anyway, so apart from an odd snide remark from him, he generally left us alone.

We have finished discussing what everyone wants to do after they finish school and are enjoying yummy ice blocks as we sit at the outdoor table under an umbrella. "Has anyone seen Alex or the others around these holidays?" I say changing the subject.

"Yeah, I saw them at the mall a few days ago. They didn't seem to be causing trouble but then I was only there for a few minutes. Was picking up some milk, that's all."

"Things have been quiet, Logan. I hope it keeps up. I guess most kids have their parents around so the bullies have to be more careful." I look at him, "I always get a bit uncomfortable when things are quiet, is it the calm before the storm?"

We all laugh nervously and continue talking about more pleasant things like what show we last watched. Still, the tingles running up my spine are making me nervous. I have a sixth sense about these things.

It's been raining for two days so we all decide to catch a movie. We meet at the cinemas at two. I see them at the same time the others do, Donovan and Parker. I can see both Jack and Logan are ready to protect us and hope nothing is going to happen. That sixth sense I have tells me otherwise.

"Look what the cat dragged in," laughs Donovan cocky as ever. "Bit of movie watching, hey kiddies?"

Logan and Jack move in front of Chloe and me, protecting us as I predicted. I whisper to them both, "Leave them, let's head into the movie."

"Oh, Mummy Ailsa is being protective. Don't worry, we're not here to cause trouble."

As Donovan says this, Parker snickers, "Not much anyway. Go and buy us some snacks and we won't trouble you."

Jack slinks around the corner as Parker is speaking. I sneak a look at what he's doing. My hand goes to my mouth as I stifle a scream. Jack, as the Jack Russel jumps out and pulls at Parker's jeans. "What the f..., get off me. What the hell is this dog doing in the cinema?" He shakes his leg but Jack holds on, growling.

I look around to find Logan gone too and then the Maine Coon cat we see at school is attacking Donovan. I head back to where Chloe is standing and push her away from them. "We have to stop this," she says. But we end up not having to do anything ...

"What is going on here? Why are these animals here?" It's the cinema manager, pimply and short, who looks like he isn't too much older than us. "Stop this, I've called security." And within minutes, two burly security guards are on the scene.

Chloe and I stand back along with other patrons who are shocked at what is happening. Some people are gawking at the cat and dog, wondering, like everyone here, how they came to be in a cinema? Some people have their phones out filming.

Suddenly, the dog and cat run off with Donovan and Parker assessing the damage to their clothes and, in Donovan's case, the scratches on his hands.

The cinema manager, whose name tag shows his name as Theodore, a geek name if ever I heard one, speaks to the security guards, "You two take these two to centre management and clean them up. I'll be up in a minute to explain to management what happened here. I hope they believe me." Then he turns to me asking if we are ok?

"Umm, we're fine now, thanks."

"Do you know what started this? Were they your pets?"

I decide not to make more trouble for those two bullies as we may also be in trouble. "I wish I knew, the dog and cat came out of nowhere." As I'm speaking with the manager, Logan and Jack return.

"Is everything ok here?" asks Logan, "we have a movie to see."

"You four head off to watch your movie, but if we could speak with you after it finishes, we'd appreciate your help."

"Sure," says Jack moving us towards cinema four where our movie is about to start.

I am stunned by what I saw and even though I didn't see Logan become a cat, I know he had something to do with this. "You two had better start explaining, I saw Jack transform into that Jack Russel. And you Logan, you are the cat, right?"

Logan looks at Jack first, then at Chloe. They both nod. He begins by clearing his throat, "We're magicals, Als. Chloe can shape shift into the Ragdoll."

I stand there, my mouth agape. I had heard all the rumours about magicals but had dismissed them, they were only rumours after all.

Logan continues, "We have to keep this secret, ok. And sorry we haven't told you earlier. The less non-magicals know about us, the better."

"Do my parents know about this? What about your parents?"

Logan explains how his parents are magicals, Jack's mother is too, but Chloe is the only magical in her family. He says his Uncle Jackson and Aunt Trudi know about the magicals but is not sure about my parents, Nigel and Athena.

"Wouldn't my parents have told me by now if they

knew?" By this time we have found our seats but keep talking because the movie hasn't started yet. We keep our voices low not only because we're in a cinema, but also, we don't want anyone hearing us. I am overwhelmed by what I'm learning. "Why am I the last to know? Aren't I part of this group?"

Chloe turns and looks at me, "Als, we were protecting you. If you knew and were bullied into telling what you know, we would not have forgiven ourselves."

"As if I would do that!" I am offended with them thinking I would betray them. "You guys know you can trust me." I start shaking, my eyes wet.

"Well, we have to now," says Jack. "We know you'll keep our secret. You also know without our animals, we are not able to fight the bullies."

The ads have finished and the movie is starting. "I know, I wish you had told me sooner though. For now, let's watch the movie, we can talk about this later." I wipe my eyes and take a breath. I'm angry with them but they had their reasons not to tell me. Now I know their secret, I can help even more with the bullies. This elevates my mood, my body tingles with the possibilities of what I can do to help all of us.

When the movie finishes I suggest we go and sit somewhere to discuss the magical situation but the cinema manager want to talk to us. I'm not really sure what we can tell him, but I decide to leave it to the three magicals in our group to do the talking.

We're with the manager for all of fifteen minutes, he is satisfied we had nothing to do with the cat and dog being at the cinema, and Logan assures him we weren't hurt by Donovan and Parker. He agreed we would leave it at that and allowed us to leave. By this time, our rides had arrived and we didn't talk any further. Now I know about my friends being magical, I have many questions to ask, all of which will have to wait until another time when no one else is around.

CHAPTER 13

LOGAN

The Jacaranda's Power

Another school year and another year of dealing with the bullies. And we've lost Als, who finished school last year. Once she knew we were magicals, she really stepped up and helped us with the bullies. She will be missed by all of us at school, but she is still part of our group – Jack, Chloe and me – so we'll still be catching up with her outside of school.

Donovan, Parker and their girlfriends have grown more menacing and because this is their last year, they intend to make it the worst yet and we geeks are worried. Donovan told us his plans the first week of school and we know he is serious.

"They are a real problem, we need to be vigilant."

"Ok, Logan. They may be more than we can handle though, those threats are scary."

"That's what they want us to feel, Aaron. But we will

stick to our plan." The bell chimes, "Talk more at lunchtime. See you all later."

"Yeah, ok." Aaron, one of our younger geek members, says this with an unconvincing tone. I'm not exactly worried but am a bit cautious of what is ahead of us.

Our social media accounts are targeted with hateful messages over the next few months. The accounts are fake but we suspect Donovan and his team are behind this.

Jack is targeted the most with malicious rumours surrounding his sexuality. Some of the things being said could only have come from one source – Matt.

Photo of Jack with pyjamas (Jack knows Matt gave Donovan this photo, Jack would never post it)

Aww, pretty boy has pretty pjs, we know what else happens in those pjs (sleep emoji, devil emoji)

Photo of Jack with me and other geeks

Pretty boy has many boyfriends. (Eggplant emoji along with others.)

Photo of Jack patting me as the Maine Coon

Aww, petting animals make you feel better? What else to you do to that cat? (Angry cat emoji)

Then they target me as well as Chloe and others –

Logan is pretty boy's bestest friend and more (love heart and sneering emoji)

Hey Chloe, in love with your cuz? (pink love emoji, laughing face)

Red hot anger stirs inside me as I read all this rubbish they are spurting about us. I organise a meeting for this afternoon asking everyone to attend at the usual park, this is important.

After school, there are only twelve geeks assembled not including me, Jack, Chloe and Als. This meeting was short notice, so not all members attend. Als is here. She comes when she can now that her university hours have kicked in. The bullies horrible actions are alienating more people, all the geeks are becoming angrier with each bullying. We have to find a way to stop the cyberbullying as well as keep to the plan we formulated before the last school holidays.

The plan hasn't changed too much from what we're already doing, we added the scare tactic of alerting teachers. Stopping them from cyberbullying is harder, although it did work for Alex and Callum. But I think this was due to them being at the end of their schooling rather than us threatening them. Even though these four we're dealing with now will soon finish school as well, they won't be as easy.

Both Miller and Scarlett didn't hold back on targeting Chloe and the other girls in our group. Using derogatory slurs like – bitches, bimbos, and posting malicious information to incite fighting. Unfortunately, some of the girls tried to fight back only to end up in tears and seeking counselling.

"Ok, rather than fight back, we need to report these attacks. Use the platform's reporting tools or block these users."

"Reporting them? What a load of crap, those reporting tools don't do anything."

"Jack, they may help more than we know. It's a start." Everyone murmurs and seem to agree with me.

"Threatening to show them up by posting what they are doing is working too. The girls have slowed down, Donovan and Parker are harder to deal with." I look around making sure everyone is still listening, then continue, "We can also report them to all the teachers as well as our principal, building this type of support network will help. Talking to our parents might help too."

A few shake their heads, they don't have that kind of

relationship with their parents. "Mine are too busy working," says Tahlia. "But I'm happy to tell the teachers, I get on better with them."

I feel sorry for Tahlia and the others telling us they can't speak to their parents about their problems, it makes me think my parents aren't that bad after all.

"Anyone else have other ideas to share?"

"How about we get them expelled? I don't know if I can take anymore of their assaults. The cyber stuff is horrible." This comes from a boy standing towards the back, I don't know him and ask his name.

"Benjamin, I'm in Year 8." He's small, I can just see the top of his head.

"Thanks, would you come up the front, please. Let's talk more about what has been happening to you." He shuffles his way to the front, his face red hot with shame, something he should not be feeling. Bullying is not the fault of the person being bullied.

"Benjamin, hi. This is a safe space, you can confide in us. Tell us what's been going on."

He clears his throat, sniffs and talks while shuffling his feet. Like Jack, he is targeted often, both physically and online. The cyberbullying has reached the point he has closed his social media accounts, this has helped with that problem. But it has made the physical attacks worse. "I fixed one thing and made the other worse. I'm no match for them and I usually give them whatever they want. I had to have my laptop replaced recently." His voice quivers and I can see how nervous and frustrated he is. Als comes up to him and whispers something, probably something comforting like *we're here to help.*

"Everyone, this is what I am talking about. See what we

need to do to stop people like Benjamin feeling like losers." I wait as people nod and agree with me.

"Benjamin," I look straight at him, "Use us when the bullies are around. Yell, scream. We will find you. The other thing you can do is try not to be on your own, have one or two of your friends with you. Remember, there is safety in numbers." The claps start slowly and then intensify. "Ok, thanks for coming everyone, see you all soon."

It's only a few days later when Benjamin is targeted by both Donovan and Parker. I can hear them telling Benjamin to handover money. As I turn the corner of the school building, I see them near the toilet block. Benjamin yells, "Don't touch me." He has seen me and even though he is frightened, he's determined to stop what is happening to him.

I text Jack and Chloe, I'm going to need their help. Our powers are strong right now, with the Jacarandas having been in bloom over the summer, we magicals sit under or in the trees when they're in full colour, replenishing our magic. We can stay transformed for hours when our powers are topped up.

Donovan and Parker look evil and menacing, they're ready to take on anyone. Slinking back around the corner so they don't see me, I transform. Jack and Chloe are behind me and they do the same. Chloe goes first and moves towards Benjamin meowing, he and the bullies look over.

"That mangy cat again. Watch out Parker, the other one and the dog are probably around too."

Chloe swiftly moves in front of Benjamin and sits. That's all she does, she sits.

"Why you ..." Donovan takes a swipe at her and then he yells. Expletives pour out of his mouth because she has given him a nasty scratch.

Jack is behind Parker and growls then barks making Parker jump. Parker is afraid of dogs and inches back towards Donovan. "Get away you dirty animal."

As I wait, I can feel the fear coming from Parker making my way around him and jump the back of Donovan's bare legs. He's wearing shorts and it's easy for me to give him a big tearing scratch down one calf.

"Crap, that bloody hurts," he says still holding the hand that Chloe had a go at.

I leave Jack the Jack Russel and Chloe the Ragdoll to sit with Benjamin, protecting him. I walk to the back of the toilet block and transform back to my human form.

I walk out and stand in front of the bullies. "You two need to get out of here before I post this vid of you bullying Benjamin." I had set up my phone to film, it wasn't good quality but they couldn't see that. I hold my phone up for them to see. "I also have the numbers of two teachers I can call. So, I think you had better go and get those scratches looked at Donovan and take your scared friend away from this dangerous dog sitting here." On cue, Jack starts barking and Donovan and Parker run. I laugh and as I look around, Jack had attracted a crowd with his barking. They are clapping.

I take a bow smiling at Chloe and Jack.

Once the crowd disperses, Chloe and Jack go out of site to transform. "Wow, that felt so good. Benjamin, are you ok?" Jack says this as they walk back towards us.

"Yes, fine now, thanks Jack."

"Ok, let's get you home," I say feeling great to have helped Benjamin who is a kid who really needed our help.

CHAPTER 14

Edward
    The Five Gets Serious

Looking around at all the magicals enjoying the sunshine, I'm aware of eyes peering at me. The Five is standing far enough away not to look suspicious, but I know they are targeting me. Wade, now the ultimate leader of the push to have me expelled from the Alliance, has let me know they have the numbers behind them to do this. "You don't belong with us and we're doing something about it," he had shouted at me during our last A-Alliance meeting. Some magicals had jeered and booed, others clapped and cheered. From what I could tell, there seemed to be an even split. I wasn't feeling good about this, my gut was telling me things were about to get worse.

The meeting this morning had gone well. Many magicals had done some good deeds and Ester congratulated Hannah on caring for two magical children who were ill. Hannah is a special kind of magical who uses her powers for the good of others. I wonder sometimes what the hell she sees in her husband, Noel.

I'm taken out of my thoughts by Wade.

"Mr Shipley, your days are numbered." He's sneering at me, standing with both hands on his hips and his four friends behind him.

I almost laugh at him calling me by my last name, no one does that here, we're all friends. Well, most of us are anyway. I look around and see there are more people gathering around, things are getting serious.

Ester, Sally, Hannah, Sally's parents Bill and Elizabeth, all come to stand behind me. Ester places her hand on my shoulder, "Wade, we've spoken about this and Edward is more than welcome to be at the A-Alliance. He has more class and magic in his little finger than you have, so I suggest we all just get on, shall we?"

"Oh poor Eddie, he needs an old crone like Ester to protect him. Watch it Ester or you'll be next."

Cringing at the diminutive of my name, I speak with my chest forward and stand tall. Feeling like I'm putting across an imposing image, I start, "Wade, you and your crew may have an issue with me but leave Ester and the others out of this. How dare you insult her, she does not deserve it. There is no need to hurl abuse at anyone other than me. Now I know Henry and Garrett started this with you, Kinley-Lee and Vera tagging along now, but Wade do you really know why you all have this vendetta against me?"

"You are not a magical born." He blurts this out with visceral disdain. "Your twin sister bestowed her magic to you when she died, we all know your story. How can you be a member of our committee, one of the highest members of the A-Alliance with inherited magic? It's utter bullshit."

Wade turns to the others and the crowd around him and they all murmur and nod their agreement.

All this negativity is seeping through the crowd, I can feel the jealously oozing out of The Five who see themselves as the ones who should be on the committee. The scowls on the faces of Kinley-Lee and Vera are terrifying, but I stand my ground. "I agree, I am not magical born, but everyone knows the story of how I came to be a committee member. Please, share your stories of what you have achieved as magical borns?" Ester pats my shoulder and whispers, "This will be interesting."

Feeling the positivity from my side of the space with my crowd behind me, my resolve is strengthening, they will not beat me down. I wait patiently for a response. "Anyone? No, not one of you has acted in kind to any non-magical?" I puff my chest out even further and Sally takes my hand, squeezing it.

"Ah, enough of this crap," yells Henry who comes to stand next to Wade. "Wadda ya all reckon is going on here? He's not a magical, that's it. It's that simple."

Wade gives Henry a severe look making Henry step back to where he was standing. "Appreciate your input, Henry," says Wade with a contemptuous inflection.

Trouble in paradise? Are there ripples of tension within The Five? This is something we can capitalise on.

Wade continues, "Edward." He pauses for effect. "Edward my man, you know deep down this is all a bit on the nose and you need to step aside before anything happens. You were born a non-magical, then on the unfortunate death of your twin sister, you became a magical. You had to learn the craft more than any of us born magicals will ever have to. Yes, you did a good deed, but so have many other magicals, me included."

"Oh really?" Ester whispers to me again.

"Many of the true magicals will know I helped a young boy who was run over by a car while riding his bike. I was the one who alerted the authorities and stayed with him until they arrived. And many other magicals have done similar acts of kindness to non-magical people." Some random claps come from behind him. From my side, there are snickers. How noble of him to help one person.

"Well, I am impressed, Wade. You helped one non-magical, once! Brilliant, well done." I clap my hands and a few others do as well. I notice some of his followers clap as well. How dim can these idiots be? "We all know the zero tolerance bullying rules at schools implemented after I received my magical powers have helped and are still helping many thousands of school students." The roar and clapping behind me is deafening and Sally tightens her grip on my hand. The euphoric feeling I was experiencing is spurring me on. "Now, the five of you need to look at what you are doing and give us more evidence of why I need to step down. When you help non-magicals in a significant way, then come and speak to the committee members. Right now you are wasting everyone's time when we should be enjoying each other's company."

Ester starts clapping this time, slowly and methodically. Others join in, each clap becoming faster. "You heard Edward, it's time to stop this nonsense. Let's get back to having a good time." She heads towards The Five, "Either join us or leave, we've all had enough of your whining."

It's Saturday night, our monthly games night, this time it's our turn to host. Sally has laid out nibbles and drinks and Jackson, Trudi, Athena and Nigel will arrive soon. Logan, Chloe and Ailsa are out doing what teenagers do.

I'm dealing out the cards as we laugh about Nigel and his antics. He's a joker from way back, telling us once again how he keeps things interesting at his office. As an FX trader, he is a finance nerd running his own consultancy.

"You all know that finance can be a dry subject and as far as my job goes, it can be. But it doesn't mean I have to be boring, does it?" We all smirk and I shrug as I finish dealing the cards. "So, this week I gave everyone a challenge to come up with an end of financial year promotion to woo more clients. And it had to be out of the ordinary, none of this free advice rubbish. And guess what, our youngest team member, an intern, came up with a good idea."

Sally laughs, "Why does that surprise you? Young people have good ideas too."

"I guess so. Anyway, he suggested that we guarantee new clients a return if they spend over a certain amount."

"What? Are you crazy," spurts out Athena. "Since when can financial returns be guaranteed?"

Nigel laughs, "We will have a disclaimer, Athena, we're not that stupid."

"You said this was funny, I'm not laughing yet."

He mimics a sad face, "No trust from my wife, hmm? I haven't got to the funny part yet. So, I asked young Liam to put together a proposal and you know what he said?" We all look towards Nigel with blank faces. "I came up with the idea, you want more? Then pay me more."

We all laugh with Athena adding, "Ha, you got played by a teenager. Liam is one smart boy."

"Yeah well, he's no longer with us, his internship finished. What have you all been up to?"

We chat amicably with each of us filling us all in with what has been happening. It's mainly general life stuff —

work, what we've enjoyed streaming, and Sally talking about her work at the library.

"It's nice to see students coming back to the library to do research rather than relying only on what's online. Many people now realise the internet is full of fake rubbish."

"That's good to hear. All that guff about books and libraries disappearing hasn't happened."

"Oh, I was worried about my job at one stage, but this is giving all librarians hope again. Imagine a world without books? And information giving us real knowledge?"

While Sally is talking we are playing cards and Nigel puts down his hand, "I win. Again." He stands and does a victory dance.

"Oh, Nigel, sit down you idiot." Athena pretends to be angry as she mocks him, but we all laugh knowing Nigel is the smartest person in the room.

The night continues with copious amounts of alcohol being consumed by all except for me, I'm the designated driver. The host remains sober in order to drive everyone home safely. It's hilarious watching everyone else being drunk and does make for an interesting evening.

I'm in the kitchen when Trudi comes in. "How are you doing? I hear The Five made a move on your position."

"They tried, but we shut it down. Ester was a great help. Although, I don't think the matter is finished, they'll keep trying."

Trudi continues asking what I'm going to do about it and we talk about my options. "Technically, The Five has a point, I wasn't born a magical." As I say this, Athena and Nigel come in to say goodbye.

"What? Did I hear you say..." Athena is stunned and Nigel is staring at me. I'm in two minds whether I deny this and say they heard this out of context, but I'm sick of them being our only friends who don't know.

"Come back to the table and I'll explain," I say ushering us all out of the kitchen.

Once we're settled back into our seats, I start telling Athena and Nigel my story. I also explain who else is a magical and why they have to keep this secret.

"I knew it, there was something about you I couldn't put my finger on. Those weird disappearances you always explained away in half-truths. Bloody hell, mate, why are Athena and I the last to know? Does Ailsa know about you all?"

I can see his anger, a vein in his neck pulsing, and Athena isn't too pleased either. "She does but was sworn to secrecy. Look, I'm sorry, but we try to keep non-magicals who know our secret to a minimum. I know we should have told you earlier, maybe at the same time as Trudi and Jackson, but ..."

"But nothing. This is bullshit! Come on Athena, we're out of here. How can we call these people friends when they've been lying to us all these years." He is up and grabs Athena's hand, pulling her off the seat.

Sally and I along with Trudi and Jackson watch them leave wondering how a lovely night has ended up with us possibly losing two good friends.

CHAPTER 15

LOGAN
Dad Worries

I sit quietly with Chloe, Tahlia and Georgia. We're waiting for Jack to join us. I pull my school parker around me, the winter chill has set in.

Tahlia, Georgia, Manuel and Aaron all know about us being magicals, we couldn't keep it from them as they sit with us often now.

"Logan. Did you hear me?"

"Huh, what?"

"Why so quiet. What's worrying you?" Chloe has a caring look on her face, reminding me of Als, who is missed by all of us.

I think about Als and her parents, how they took the news about us being magicals. This news didn't go down well with Athena and Nigel when they found out, they didn't speak to my parents or Trudi and Jackson until the next games night. That is the longest time these friends had not spoken. My mum talked to them and they resolved their issues with life being stable again. Well, mostly. Nigel still shows his anger whenever the subject is brought up.

"I'm worried about my dad, he's being targeted again at the Alliance. He has been quiet these past months." Jack arrives and hears what I've said.

"Yeah, The Five are getting brutal. They've spread rumours and stupid lies." He sits and looks at me with a worried look.

"We need to help him. Jack, can you talk to your mother, she'll know what to do?"

"Sure. Anyone else have ideas? Chloe?"

"Well, my parents are technically not part of the Alliance, but I'll talk to them. Oh, here comes trouble." We look over to the oval and see Donovan, Parker and their girlfriends heading our way.

This is all I need, I'm worried enough about my father, I really don't want to deal with these fools.

"Oh look, here's the geeks no one likes."

"It's the other way round, Donovan."

He look towards Jack who had said this. "Especially you, Jack. No one likes you!" Donovan's face is up against Jack's, he's crouching on his knees so he can eye Jack menacingly.

"Get off me, you wanker. Your breath reeks."

Donovan is stunned for a minute then his crazy laugh bellows out. "The littlest geek thinks he has power."

We stand our ground while the four of them keep laughing. They think they're so great turning every geek's life at this school into a nightmare. Zero tolerance, what a joke!

Jack the Jack Russel appears in front of me, I had wondered why Jack had gone quiet. He's growling, showing his teeth. For a small dog, cute even, with his white coat sporting one brown spot, brown eyes and an elegant, angular face, he is frightening when he's angry.

"Oh, I'm so scared." Donovan fakes this by waving his hands around. Then he sends a kick Jack's way who proceeds to grab Donovan's grey school pant by the hem. Throwing his head about, he rips off a piece of fabric. Spitting it out he barks and heads for Donovan's other leg.

Parker decides to become involved by trying to pick up ... "You stupid dog," he yells as his attempt to grab misses Jack.

We're all surprised Parker has the guts to be near the Jack Russell let along go for him.

Jack runs towards the girlfriends who scream while Donovan ambles up to me. "Call off your hound or I might be inclined to cause some injury to one of you." I stare at him calling Jack to "come back." He does as he's told but is still menacing them with his growling.

We're saved once again by the bell, lunch is over. We wait until the bullies are far enough ahead of us before we head back to our classrooms. Jack remains behind to transform then follows us.

I walk in the front door hearing my dad's voice. What is he doing home at this time? Placing my backpack down, I say, "Hi, I'm home."

"Hi, Logan. We'll be down in a minute."

That was my mum and in less than a minute, she's in the kitchen with me. "Did I hear Dad's voice?"

"Yes, he's home. Ester is coming over with your grandparents and Hannah to discuss shutting down The Five once and for all."

I'm glad to hear this and only nod. Words won't form as

I've been emotionally invested in trying to think of how to help with this situation.

"Come here sweetheart, I know you've been worried too." She pulls me to her and I snuggle into her shoulder by bending my head down. Either she is shrinking or I've had another growth spurt.

Calmness envelopes my body as I stay in her arms.

Pulling way, I sniff. "If dad is banished it affects all of us. How do we show our heads at the Alliance? It would be too embarrassing. And if The Five come to power, I don't think I'd want to be a part of the A-Alliance at all."

Dad comes into the kitchen and agrees. "It would not be beneficial for any magical if The Five are part of the committee. And it's not going to happen, believe me." He places his hand on my shoulder and I feel calmer still. After another frustrating day at school, my parents have the power to make me feel safe.

"Is it ok if I sit in on the meeting?"

"No homework this afternoon, Logan?" asks Mum.

"My last period was a free one, I've finished what I need to do." Mum looks over to Dad who nods. Calmness and relief wash over me, I know there is a solution to this mess now, my father won't be expelled.

An hour later we're all seated in our lounge room, Dad is standing up with Ester and she is talking. "We're putting this to a vote, we've all had enough of this nonsense. Every magical, including the ones overseas, will vote, it's compulsory. Like Edward, I can't see a future for the Alliance if The Five group is on the committee."

"That would be disastrous, imagine all the infighting, which is already happening between them now." I look over at my grandfather, who is showing concern, his face stern yet worried.

"That's right, Bill. And they would not be fair leaders either, there will be dark days ahead if Edward is expelled and we are left with that lot. So, I will organise for the vote to go ahead on the first of next month. Are you all willing to help with this organisation and with the counting?" We all nod, me included. My body is finally relaxing for the first time in months, my shoulders are not around my ears any longer.

"Ok, then it's settled. I'll start with a roster of jobs, Sally and Elizabeth, if you would please get the word out with announcements once the roster is out. Edward, you had better lie low for now, we don't want you being attacked before this vote can go ahead."

"Will do, Ester. Although, they will keep sending out untruths, maybe more so once they know about the vote."

"Probably, Edward, but the vote will be final. I'm confident it will go our way."

My parents see everyone out and breathe a sigh of relief. I couldn't see how my mother and I could have remained part of the A-Alliance without Dad being there. The vote will go our way, I want to be as confident as Ester.

CHAPTER 16

JACK
A Bully's Revenge

I'm sitting with Logan, Chloe and a few of the other geeks at lunch when I see Donovan and the other three heading our way. Parker is next to Donovan with Miller and Scarlett lagging behind.

"Jack, be careful. Donovan is pissed at you for what happened yesterday. I knew there would be come back," says Chloe.

I smile as I remember the feeling of success after yesterday's debacle with these two boofheads. They may be street smart, but that is where their intelligence ends. I felt elated with a sense of achievement after what happened. This feeling spurs me on every time we have a win against them. They tried to bully me after school not realising two teachers were walking up behind them. We all started laughing and anger sizzled in both of them because they couldn't work out why we were laughing.

When Donovan threw a punch at me, the teachers quickly shut things down. The last thing we saw was Donovan leering at us and mouthing, "This isn't finished," as the teachers handed out detention. I guess I'm about to find out it isn't finished.

"Jacky, Jacky, Jacky." Donovan spurts this version of my name out slowly, he's menacing and Parker is doing his best to emulate him. I try not to laugh because Parker looks awkward, not menacing. "You should have warned us the teachers were walking behind and could see what was happening. For this you will pay." He is close enough for me to smell his foul breath.

"Donovan, there are teachers around now, they're on duty. I'd be careful if I was you."

"Shut up, Logan. I'm not stupid. This is just a warnin'. We'll be on our way. For now." He turns walking away flicking us the finger. The other three follow him. I'm sure I see relief wash over Parker's face as they walk away.

"Jack, you had better be careful over the next few days, who knows when they're going to strike. Make sure to be with someone at all times."

"Thanks Mumma Chloe, I'll be sure to do that." I adore Chloe but sometimes her mothering, which she has taken on since Als left, gets on my nerves. She's always stating the bleeding obvious. We geeks always stay in pairs, or in groups because it's safer. And our group knows to keep an eye out of anything the bullies are up to.

"You need to be extra careful, Donovan is out for revenge. He's angry about getting detention for the whole week."

"He should have gotten more. What if that punch had landed? I would have been knocked out."

"Yes, probably. We should all be more vigilant." Chloe

finishes her speech as she heads into her classroom, I'm the last one to enter my classroom.

The days pass without incident and I'm a bit more relaxed. My mind isn't always thinking about those idiots. Sitting with Logan in his room after school, we're battling each other on a video game.

"Things have been quiet, I wonder what's going on with them?"

"Maybe the detention taught Donovan something?"

"Yeah, right Jack. I'm sure he's seen the light and become a model citizen," I laugh. "No, he's biding his time waiting for his best opportunity."

"I'm sick of him targeting me out of our group. Not that I want him to hurt any of you, but I've had enough. It felt good to laugh at them that day and he deserved to get detention." Logan remains quiet because he's concentrating on the game. I know he feels bad I'm bullied the most, but it's because I'm an easy target, especially that I'm gay. No one else cares but the bullies take advantage of it. But, when I'm Jack the Jack Russell, well then I have the power I need.

I'm what the girls call *petite* for a boy, smaller than most boys my age and I look younger too. Puberty hasn't hit me yet and at almost 15 years old I'm wondering when it will. Logan's upper lip has spurted some dark hairs, although he hasn't grown anything under his arms yet. We're both slow in the puberty stakes. Another thing the bullies latch onto.

"Mate, what are you doing? Get out of there, you're about to be killed."

Logan pushes me from my thoughts as I fight to regain my place in the game. I wish school was just a game.

We all pull our parkas around us shielding us from the

vicious southerly buster that picked up with the storm. Logan is waiting for his mother, I'm waiting for my father and Als and Chloe have already been picked up. Logan and I are talking when we hear Donovan's voice.

"The two boyfriends cuddlin' up. How cute." He ambles up to us with Parker as always, next to him. "Well, well, it has been a few weeks so I think it's time we settled things, hey pretty boy?" Before I know it, his fist hits my face, I feel his slamming knuckles on my cheek. The crack is loud.

A teacher walks up after I'm punched. "What the hell is going on here?" A female teacher is walking towards us. "Jack, you're hurt. Has one of you called an ambulance?" When we just look stunned, she pulls out her phone and calls one. Donovan and Parker start to walk away. "Don't you even think about it. Stop right there." Her voice is stern and has authority, making the two bullies stop in their tracks.

I'm lying on the damp grass agony leeching through my face, I feel like my cheek has doubled in size. Logan is crouched next to me asking me to be patient, the ambulance is on its way.

The teacher had called both parents of the bullies, who were on their way too. I hear two cars pull up and see my mum running towards us. "Not again! Jack, oh no, your face."

"Hannah, I'm so sorry, but these two will be dealt with." Behind her is Logan's dad who walks over to Logan and places his arm around him.

Mum has knelt down touching my face gently. "Thanks, I appreciate that. But this has to stop, what do you two have to say for yourselves?" Donovan and Parker shrug, their faces showing their stupidity – blank and bland.

"Enough. You two will definitely be dealt with, I will be speaking with the principal personally." Edward's face is stern, I've seen him this angry before and he has been able to use his influence, Donovan and Parker have gone too far this time.

The ambulance arrives and I'm taken to hospital with my mother following in our car.

CHAPTER 17

Edward
Unexpected Assistance

We're all seated in the courtroom. Along with me are Sally, Ester, Hannah, Bill, Elizabeth and a number of other magicals who offered to help us with the vote. Ester has handed out the voting forms and is talking about how the online site can be accessed only by magicals. "Please give as many of these voting forms out as you are able to, anyone from overseas will access the online form. Everyone is welcome to vote whichever way is more convenient for them." Ester indicates to me to take the floor.

I head towards Ester who is behind the lectern, but I remain slightly to the left with my right hand on it, standing tall and with as much authority as I can muster, I start. "Thank you all for being here in support of me, it means a lot. We are unified by the need to stop The Five from dividing us, to stop their lies and innuendo. A future with The Five on the committee is abhorrent to me. And I'm sure to all of you in this courtroom. Their infighting is already apparent, imagine this when they have the power of being on the committee? We are to avoid such an outcome at all costs if we are to keep the A-Alliance secret and working to help the non-magicals, not hinder them." Applause and shouts of "yes" swell throughout the room as tears well in my eyes. What will I do if I lose the vote, I cannot imagine my life without these wonderful people who have taken me in.

Breathing in and stopping the tears, I continue to address them, reiterating some of the things Ester has already spoken of and talk with emotion about what this all means to me. How the A-Alliance has given meaning to my life, how I met my wife here … Sally comes and stands with me … how I learned more about magic and how to harness its power here, how the sense of community here influences the way I do things. "I have so much to be thankful for and know you all will do everything in your power to keep me (and my family) here."

"Hear, hear." Ester is standing with me too now and is applauding as enthusiastically as the others in the room. Bill, Elizabeth and Hannah join us. We join hands and raise them in unison, we are going to win this vote.

Heading out into the meadow, the crisp winter air is calm, hopefully this is a good omen. A table is bulging with food and drinks as we all mingle and chat. Hannah walks up towards me and raises a glass, "To Edward Shipley, you have my vote."

"Thanks Hannah, your support has never wavered."

"I'm frightened to think about what will happen if The Five wins this. I can imagine what horrors they will bestow on us. Jack will be targeted, I'm sure. And coming here without you, Sally and Logan being here, is unimaginable."

"I try not to think about not being able to come here, my brain won't let me see that scenario. We are in the hands of all the magicals worldwide now, I hope we have done enough to convince them that those bullies cannot take over."

Sally comes up and joins us. "Hi Hannah, I too appreciate you being here. Does Noel know where you are, it is Sunday after all?"

"I told him I needed to go and care for someone in the city and I would be a few hours. He knows I do volunteer work for the elderly. It is unusual I do this on a Sunday but he didn't query it."

I indicate we make ourselves comfortable at the table, I'm beginning to feel weary, my emotions have been giving me jolts for months.

"Will you ever tell Noel about being magical? Especially that Jack is one too."

"Believe me Sally, I have thought about it many times. But ... he has said some awful things about magicals over the years. Remember when Leafia the Goblin caused all that commotion years ago, well he was livid about being made to look like a fool when he told everyone he saw a goblin. He told me the whole story. Well, the things he said he would do to Leafia if he saw her again I don't want to repeat. Honestly, it was brutal." Hannah finishes and the house alarm peals, alerting us an intruder has entered the house. Hannah puts her hand to her mouth when she sees her youngest son walking towards us.

Matt stares at his mother, "I knew there was something going on with you."

"What the hell are you doing here? How did you know where I was?"

"You've been going out a lot Mum. Dad has been

murmuring about how he wonders what the hell you are up to. So, I followed you today. I wasn't sure how to get into this place, but when someone left, I managed to throw myself into the hall before the door shut. This place is beyond awesome by the way, look at those incredible animals. How could you keep something like to from Dad and me?"

Hannah's face goes into loving mother mode and she stretches out her arms asking him to come to her. "Matt, your father isn't going to accept me and Jack being magicals. You must not tell him. And how did you follow me here? Our home is a good hour's walk away."

"Please listen to your mother," pleads Ester.

"I rode my bike. And no way, Dad needs to know what you're up to. You should trust your own husband. This magical stuff is dangerous, people are suspicious of you lot."

We all join in pleading with him but he seems determined to out us.

"Look, let me talk to your father. If he accepts us, both Jack and I, then we can keep it quiet and within our family."

"Jack! That little runt is a magical. What the ..."

"Please, Matt, listen to me and all of us here. Don't do something rash and ruin what we have here. Magicals do not harm anyone, in fact, we help the non-magicals. Look at the law Edward had passed in schools, the Zero Tolerance rule."

"That was you, Mr Shipley? Not that the bullies take any notice of that rule. I see what they do to Jack, Mum."

"Yes, and from what Jack tells me you're not any help."

"Not my problem."

"You ungrateful boy." Hannah is visibly upset and Sally goes up to calm her. She places her arm around Hannah's shoulder.

"Enough, Matt. You've caused a real stir here today. Let your mother speak to your father before you cause more problems. We do not need to be outed to the non-magicals, you will be hurting all of us, including your mother and brother."

Hannah looks at her son urging him to behave. She places her hands on his shoulders, "Think about what will happen if the non-magicals learn about us. There will be jealously, division and many will suffer."

I move towards Matt saying, "Be the better man here, Matt. Don't do anything foolish."

Matt's shoulders droop, his face softens. "I was worried about you Mum, I wanted to know where you were." Hannah's face softens too as tears move down her face. She brings him to her, hugging him.

Relief washes over me, it seems we have convinced Matt for now. He and Hannah leave after a few minutes with us all hoping Matt can keep his mouth shut.

Watching my computer screen with anticipation, the numbers for me to remain are encouraging. It's too close to call yet, but I'm cautiously optimistic. Having spoken with many magicals over the past week since the voting forms went out, they all said they were giving me their vote. But, until the voting closes at the end of the month, I really don't know which way it will fall. Three more weeks to go.

I stand and stretch, I've been working on invoices and quotes for hours. Closing my laptop, my stomach grumbles, I didn't eat lunch. Heading towards the kitchen I hear Sally and Logan talking.

"Well, you've decided to come out of your hole," laughs Sally.

"Sorry you two, I had a lot of work to catch up on. With

the vote taking up all my spare time these past months, I neglected my work. Contractors were screaming to be paid."

"Dad, Mum was telling me about Matt. I haven't heard anything around school, so I guess he didn't open his big mouth."

"I hope he doesn't, Hannah was quite upset about Matt showing up like that. It's been a week, so maybe he will do as he promised. I'm starving, what's for dinner?"

"We ordered take out, hope you feel like Thai."

"Sally, right now I'd eat anything. Thai is fine."

"It will be here in ten minutes, Logan help set the table please." Sally busies herself getting cutlery and plates out then whispers to me, "We need to talk after dinner."

"Huh, what's going on?" I whisper back wondering why she doesn't want Logan to hear.

"It's about the vote. Can't talk now."

Having checked the stats before closing my laptop, I'm wondering what the problem is. But my stomach tells me to worry about eating first.

With Logan having gone up to his room, Sally walks into the lounge room. "Drink?"

"I feel like I'm going to need one. Yes please."

She returns with two scotches and hands one to me. Sitting next to me, she begins. "Ester has heard The Five has been spreading more vicious rumours about you, she's worried."

"What more can they say? What devious deeds have I done this time?"

Sally laughs lightening the mood a little. "She didn't go into what they're saying, but she is worried the undecided magicals are being targeted."

"I checked the numbers before dinner, we have a slight lead. It's too early to tell. But it is a problem because those who haven't decided whether they want me on the committee can be swayed."

"Exactly, we may need to do something. Maybe send a message to all magicals from you, we need to market you better."

I feel uncomfortable being made into a commodity but Sally had a point. "Let me speak to Ester tomorrow, we can work on something together."

Sally leans into me and sighs with relief. "Cheers to this working in our favour."

The next three weeks are horrible, my nerves on high alert and even though the message was sent out, the numbers didn't move much. The slight lead was eroded away, but much to my surprise, we received unexpected help. Leafia.

CHAPTER 18

Edward
The Vote is Counted

At work and concentrating on plans laid out in front of me, I hear the door of the demountable office open. It's Noel.

"Hi."

"Don't you *hi* me. You were that mangy cat that gave me grief at school, you're a magical like my wife and son." Noel's ruddy complexion shows I should be worried as he spits out these words. "What have you been up to with my wife?"

Stunned, I'm not quite sure what he's accusing me of. "Listen, firstly, hello Noel, and secondly, I hope you're not accusing me of what I think you are?"

"Bullshit, Hannah has been spendin' more time with you than me over the past months and I don't trust you. I don't bloody well trust her either, how dare she lie to me for all this time. My marriage is a sham."

I can't believe what I'm hearing, "You don't trust me?

What the hell are you talking about, you bullied me at school, I was protecting myself."

"Yeah, by using your magic. How could I compete with that? And you stay away from my wife."

"Noel, there is nothing between Hannah and me. I'm happily married and I assume Hannah is too. She was only protecting you."

"From what? Your magic. I can tell you I'm more than hurt right now learning this secret years into our marriage." He turns towards the door, "This is a warning Edward, don't mess with my family or your little secret will be broadcast by Matt and me. We're both pissed about being lied to."

Feeling for him I understand how awful that must have been, but he needs to see reason. "As we all told Matt, outing us magicals will cause more problems than it solves. Please think about how this will affect your family. And I promise, Hannah and I have not done anything wrong, she loves you. Why would I come between you two?"

Opening the door, he scowls at me, "Who knows how you magicals think? Maybe our rules don't mean anything to you because you can use your magic to bend them." I try to answer but he slams the door behind him.

Arriving home, Sally is bringing in the washing and I help her with it. She sees the look on my face and knows I'm upset. I tell her about Noel's visit.

"You and Hannah? Oh that's laughable."

"Well, I can see his point. He did mention Hannah has been spending more time with me than him, which is true."

"With us and other magicals, not you on your own. I'll speak to Hannah, I'm sure she will calm him down."

"Probably, but we need to keep a lid on this because

both Noel and Matt can blurt our secret out at any time. As if the vote isn't enough, I've had it!"

"Stay calm, worrying about both the vote and what Noel and Matt will do won't change things. Come on, help me with dinner, it will take your mind off things."

As we prepare dinner, we continue discussing the vote, which thanks to Leafia's help, is edging our way again. Leafia had organised the goblin community to spread the word about keeping me on the committee. Unfortunately, they are not able to vote because they are non-human magicals, but they have the numbers to change things for us. They targeted the magicals who were yet to decide.

"Ester tells me Leafia is doing a great job and the figures show it. This gives me hope."

"Oh good. That's one less thing to worry about. Although, I've been confident we will win, I believe in you. Call Logan please, let's eat."

As I head to Logan's room, I'm happy she believes in me, but is it enough?

Voting has ended and we're all in the courtroom again, doors sealed, so we can tally all the written forms. The online votes show us with a slight lead again. Not enough to make me feel comfortable though. If the voting isn't conclusive, The Five will be on the war path giving us grief again.

The silence is filled with anticipation as we are all heads down and calculating. I'm shaking despite the room being warm and I know anxiety when I feel it. My right leg twitches as

Sally places her hand on my thigh to calm me and whispers, "We have hours ahead of us, please stay calm. Remember, we are leading."

We are and I must keep thinking it will increase. We

have to win this. Breathing deeply I concentrate on counting the votes.

Three hours later we emerge from the courtroom. Ester is the only one who knows the result, she was collating the final votes we all handed her. "Everyone go home and relax. The hard work is done. I will call an extraordinary meeting for Wednesday night, two nights from now. The result will be announced then."

Two more days to wait. My brain won't shut off, how the hell am I going to sleep?

CHAPTER 19

LOGAN
A Solution

I'm walking out of my double science class with Jack. The wind chills me through even though I have my parker on. Being anxious about the vote that will be announced tomorrow night, my body is responding by winding me tight, the rigidity keeping me from functioning.

"There is not much more we can do, Logan. Worrying isn't helping you."

We walk towards the road outside school waiting for our mothers to arrive. "I know but it's hard, I don't want to think about a vote that doesn't go my father's way. What does your mother think?"

"She's been quiet since Dad found out about us. He walks around muttering how she should have been honest with him (and Matt). What he doesn't realise is this is the reason she didn't tell him, she knew he would react like the idiot that he is."

I'm stunned with Jack's comment about his father, he has never said anything bad about him. "Don't take it all out on your father, he has every right to be angry."

"Yeah, I know. It sucks to be in our house right now." His mother drives up and he moves towards the car, "See you tomorrow, Logan."

"Bye, Jack." I watch as they drive off and within minutes my mum arrives. *It sucks being in our house too, Jack. And it has been like this for too long.*

Later, we're in the school library, it's too cold to sit outside.

"I was starving, couldn't wait for lunchtime so I ate my sandwich in class."

"How Jack? Didn't the teacher see you?"

"Nah, I took a bite each time she turned her back. Besides, I wolfed it down in a couple of bites. Any of you got anything to share, I'm still hungry."

"Boys," mutters Chloe, "here have my apple, I don't feel like it."

Jack laughs, "Ugh healthy. I was thinking of something more substantial, but thanks."

"You two should eat healthier, the junk you eat is disgusting."

"Oh come on Chloe, we're growing boys and need our energy."

"Energy comes from eating healthy food, Jack," answers Chloe. "How can you boys eat chips and burgers all the time?"

"Umm, because they taste great! Not like this apple." Chloe rolls her eyes.

I'm half listening in on this banter not really interested because I'm still counting down the hours until tomorrow night and the announcement of the voting result. Then the bell rings and it's time for class, which will take my mind off it for the next few hours.

The three of us and Manuel are walking out of the gate when Matt, who is standing near it, stops us. "So, what are you guys going to do to stop my dad and me spilling the secret?" He holds his head high with hands on hips as if we're supposed to be intimidated. He may be taller and bulkier than Jack, but Matt is no bully. We're not frightened of him.

"Back off you idiot, you're full of it." Jack walks towards his brother nudging his shoulder with force.

"I'm serious," says Matt rubbing his shoulder. "I will spill if you guys don't do as I say and give me what I want."

"And what is that?" asks Logan.

"I want to be part of the Alliance, the thing you are all a part of."

"What? Not me, I'm non-magical like you. We're not allowed to be part of the magical community, what makes you think they'll let you in?" asks Manuel, sarcasm dripping from his mouth.

"My mistake, but the three of you are." He points to me, Jack and Chloe. "You're the dark coloured cat; bro, you're that yappy Jack Russel and Chloe, you're the Ragdoll. I want to be a part of the magical society, it's cool."

Jack is about to answer when their mother arrives. "Matt don't do anything stupid. Let's discuss this at home. And not in front of our olds, just you and me."

We say our goodbyes as each of our rides arrive. I text Jack to message me later to discuss what Matt intends to do. As I enter our car, Mum asks how my day was. "Yeah, fine." I'm not feeling like talking because now there are two things to worry about, the vote and our secret being put out there.

It's ten at night and Jack and me are still talking about Matt's demands. We've been on the phone for an hour.

Jack yawns, "Man, I'm beat. Between talking Matt down and discussing his madness with my mum, and now with you ... we're not going to solve this tonight."

"No, you're right. Matt's demands are dangerous, but it might be best to wait until the vote comes through tomorrow night and then deal with him."

"Yeah, we're going to need numbers behind us to stop him. He's a problem because he has my dad behind him, they're both still pissed."

I sigh and push deeper into my pillow trying to relax, which is ridiculous because I'm too wound up. "You know, I get it. Being lied too sucks, but can you imagine the chaos if the non-magicals find out about us?"

Jack stifles another yawn, "Maybe, maybe not. Look at it this way, if our secret is out there, won't there be acceptance eventually?"

I think about what Jack is saying for a split second, then answer, "That's wishful thinking, we'll all be burned at the stake." I hear him laugh and yawn at the same time.

"Logan, we're not in the Middle Ages. Now, I gotta go, see you tomorrow."

"Yeah ok. Night, Jack." Clicking off the call, I place my phone on my bedside table and lie back down thinking about what is happening. We seem to have the bullies under control to a point, they're not a relentless since breaking Jack's cheek, but now there's the issue of Matt and his threats. And the vote. My mind races between these two issues, which have major implications to all our lives.

I roll onto my side and try to fall asleep, trying to quiet my mind. Taking a few deep breaths, I'm slowly drifting when I realise there may be a solution to stop Matt right under our nose, but it all depends on the vote.

CHAPTER 20

Edward
It's Time

Trudi is sitting with me in my lounge room. Sally and Logan have gone out leaving us alone to talk. I have reached out to Trudi many times, who is ultimately still my sounding board and has been since school, so she's popped in to sort me out.

She has her hand on my shoulder, which is stooped, my head down. "Edward, you have to stop beating yourself up, the vote will be what it will be."

Sighing, I raise my head to look at her, "I know, but the thought of The Five winning is ... shit, I don't even want to think about it." Turning towards her I continue, "You know when we were at school, I thought the bullies were the worst thing that would happen to us." I shake my head wanting to throw that thought out of my brain.

"Life isn't that simple. All of us have stuff to deal with,

being bullied was one of the things, and you know what? I think it made us better people."

"Ha, that's one way of looking at it. I wouldn't be in the position I'm in at the Alliance if I hadn't been bullied and the No Tolerance rule wasn't implemented in schools. Thanks, you've made me feel better already. Sally made a chocolate cake, how about I make us coffees and we devour it?"

"Oh yes, I'm up for that. I love Sally's famous chocolate cakes. I'm always keen for some."

We continue chatting and reminiscing as I prepare our coffees. Trudi too has days where the affect the bullying had on her puts her in a mood where she doesn't want to talk and wants to be on her own. "I know that feeling, Trudi. I've felt like that for months, wanting to crawl up into a ball and hiding from the world."

"The Five is a lot to deal with. They're essentially trying to cancel you and change your life forever. And I see your issue with them being on the committee, there would be real trouble ahead." Trudi knows as much about the magical world as I do, she has supported me since the day I told her my secret. We have had many long conversations about the happenings at the Alliance. "Is Sally worried too?"

"Both she and Logan. The only one who doesn't seem worried is Ester, which gives me hope she may know something we don't."

"It's good you arrived home early today, you need to be in the right mindset for the result tonight. You're all going right?"

"Of course, Sally and Logan along with all my other supporters, will be there. Knowing they have my back has made things easier, but ..."

"Ok, none of the negatives, I don't want to hear you talk like that. Tonight go and hold you head high whatever the outcome."

I set our coffees and the cake down on the dining table. We sit and the cake, each wanting more than one piece. "Thanks, Trudi, I appreciate you coming over. What does Jackson think about all this?"

"Oh, he said to tell you that you have his full support. If only we could vote too."

"I appreciate that, thanks. Having good friends like you two is priceless."

"Being part of this with you, for both of us, has been amazing. My friendship with you has grown strong over the years, I'll always have your back, Edward."

I nod, "Thanks, Trudi. I've always known that but it's good to hear you say it." I lick my fingers after three pieces of cake, leaving two small pieces for Sally and Logan.

"Well, I'm off. You're ok on your own?"

"Sure, I'm fine. Sally and Logan will be back soon, we need to be at the Alliance by 7pm."

"Ok, love you." Trudi stands up as I do and we hug each other, "tell Sally that cake lives up to the hype as always." At the door, she turns and says, "You've got this Edward Shipley, you know how to handle bullies." Holding the door, I smile as she walks out to her car. I muster all my strength and hope the vote goes my way tonight.

"Calm down. Everyone, a bit of shush, please."

Ester is at the lectern, the gavel reverberating against it as she slams it down. "I call this extraordinary meeting of the A-Alliance open. I'm not going to keep you all in suspense for much longer, but I need to inform you all that whatever happens tonight, the vote is final as voted by magicals the world over." Looking towards The Five, "this means you five will abide by whatever the outcome is and should you be allowed onto our committee, you will also abide by our rules and regulations as they have been since time immortal."

I scoff at this hoping for the better outcome and me staying on the committee. Sally is next to me and holds my hand as Ester announces the result.

"The No vote, meaning that Edward Shipley is to leave the A-Alliance, 46%." People begin shifting in their seats and whispers fill the air. "The Yes vote, meaning Edward Shipley remains on the committee, 52%." The room erupts with applause, Sally hugs me and Logan lets out a whoop along with many of my supporters. Ester is still speaking but not many of us take note of her saying "2% undecided."

Looking towards where The Five – Henry, Garrett, Wade, Kinley-Lee and Vera – are seated and shiver as they stare down at me with dagger faces. With a whoosh of his coat, Henry leads them out of the courtroom. What worries me now is will they listen to Ester and leave things alone, and, with 46% of votes against me, I have a lot of work to do to regain the confidence of all those magicals.

CHAPTER 21

JACK

Matt Feels the Wrath

We're all hanging out for the school year to end, the assignments and exams seem endless. I've been helped by Logan with my English ones, for some reason what is in my head doesn't translate to my assignments. My tenses are all over the place. My other problem is my stupid brother and his threats to reveal our secret. Since the vote, we've been able to keep him quiet by involving both our fathers. Although, my dad wants in as much as Matt. "Your father was brilliant at calming Matt down yesterday, Logan." Both he and I have a free period and are in the library. Technically we should be studying, but we've spent the past twenty minutes trying to sort this out.

"Yeah, he's brilliant at solving problems. But Matt and your dad want to be part of the A-Alliance so this is still a problem."

"Yep. And Matt is being as stubborn as an Ox. Ha, I

told him he looked like one and did he get pissed!" Jack laughs with force and receives a look from the librarian. He snickers, "Oops, I'd better keep it down."

"With both of them wanting in, it's making it more diffi-cult to shut this down. Dad has been busy repairing what The Five did, he and the committee members have managed to bring some no voters back into the fold. That vote was too close. Look, we need something to threaten or frighten Matt into keeping his mouth shut."

We're both silent for a bit as we think about this. "I know, what if we threaten something he enjoys? You know, threaten to take it away. Like, I could ask my parents to take his phone away."

"Why would your dad agree to that? I can understand your mother agreeing, but no, we need something more substantial than that." Again, we remain quiet as we think.

"Actually, I'm remembering something. When Matt first threatened with this, you and I talked late one night, remember that?" Jack nods. "As I was falling asleep I thought of something ... but what was it?" I wrack my brain wishing I had written it down.

"Oh yeah, I got it. We could make Matt look like he's crazy if he reveals the secret. When your father claimed he saw a goblin everyone thought he was crazy and didn't believe him. I can't see Matt wanting anyone thinking he's crazy."

I sit up straight, "Umm, that could work. He doesn't have many friends but I'm sure he wants to keep the few he has. And now that Dad knows about us magicals, he's brought up that story a few times. He's still burnt about it."

"Yeah, my dad said everyone thought he was nuts. Ok then, that's settled. Let's threaten Matt with this crazy idea later, we only have half an hour before the bell goes."

"Yeah, great. Let me do it, Logan. I can scare him and threaten him with more if he doesn't take the bait."

Being a Friday there is a mass exodus of students as soon as the bell goes. Logan and I are waiting at the side gate where Matt prefers to walk out of the school grounds. He's walking towards us and almost bumps into us, his head down in his phone.

"Fu ... you scared the shit out of me."

"You're walking while staring at your phone, you idiot. Your fault not ours. Anyway, Logan and I need to speak to you. About the Alliance ..."

"Yeah, what about it?" Matt interrupts.

"We were thinking you should go ahead and make the claim about us magicals."

"Bullshit, you're not going to let me (and Dad) into the Alliance?"

"Matt, you know you're both non-magicals, we can't let randoms in with no magic."

"We're not randoms, Jack, we're family."

"You know what we mean," I say looking at Logan who nods in agreement. "Look, go ahead and try telling everyone about our secret, how many people do you think will believe you? If anything, you'll be labelled as crazy, just like Dad was many years ago."

Matt is speechless, his head bobbing between looking at me and then Logan. "No they wouldn't. Would they?"

I decide to grab at that bit of uncertainty. "Dad was labelled as crazy when he told everyone he saw a goblin."

"Yeah, but he was telling the truth. I will be too. You two are full of shit, you don't scare me."

Logan's father arrives to pick him up. Edward rolls down the window, "Everything ok boys?" Matt is standing close to Jack with a menacing look. "Do you need me to help sort things for you?"

"It's ok Dad, brotherly spat that's all. See you Monday, Jack. Message me later."

"Yeah, sure. Thanks Mr Shipley, we're good." I watch as they drive off and then continue hassling my little brother, "Are you really going to risk being labelled crazy? I know I wouldn't allow that to happen to me." Matt is quiet, so again, I seize the moment. "You have a few years left at this school, you'll be ridiculed, I wouldn't risk it if I was you."

He doesn't answer and starts walking away. "Hey, where are you goin'? Mum will be here soon."

"Walkin' home. Can't stand being around you."

He has turned the corner by the time our mum has driven up. As I open the door she asks, "Where's Matt?"

"He's walking home."

"What? In this heat."

"Leave him alone Mum, he's shitty with me."

"So what else is new? What have you done now?" I explain the situation. "Oh, he's still threatening then. Let me talk to him when he gets home, you make yourself scarce when I do. I don't want you intimidating him."

"Fine Mum. You had better get Dad on our side too, if he still wants to be in the Alliance, Matt has more power with Dad supporting him." She looks towards me and nods. How she's going to convince my father to not want to be part of the Alliance, I don't know.

CHAPTER 22

LOGAN
  Matt's Big Mouth

With only a couple of weeks left until the Christmas holidays, we're all keen to finish assignments and get on with our summer break. All of us magicals have had our powers replenished by the Jacarandas being in bloom, I feel energised and even more so because my father is still on the committee. Although, The Five are still rumbling according to my parents. There isn't much I can do about that so I push it to the back of my mind.

After school, Jack and I are spending some time around his pool discussing how stupid his little brother is. The idiot has blabbed about having a secret to his friends, who, of course, have told others. So far Matt hasn't revealed the whole secret, but we're not taking any chances. He has given snippets about the secret changing all our lives and has told Jack multiple times that unless he and their father are allowed to be part of the A-Alliance - and soon - he will tell the world about us magicals. It's obvious to everyone who knows about us magicals that we can't let our secret escape into the world.

At lunch a few days later, Chloe, Tahlia and Georgia are putting in their thoughts as to what we should do. "That little turd has no right to be in the Alliance. I can't be there so why should he?"

Chloe laughs, "Hmm, do I note you are a bit upset about Matt, Tahlia? Although, I don't blame you. You know … Jack and Logan, your suggestion that he spill the secret and everyone thinking he's nuts, is a good one. There will be a few people who will believe him but most will know he's crazy."

I'm sitting next to Tahlia in the shade and give her a nudge. "Upset hey? Is Matt getting to you too?"

She laughs but more at the fact I've nudged her. Red-faced, she looks down at her arm smiling. "This has the potential to cause a lot of damage. People can be cruel when they don't understand something. And magic … well it's a whole other world."

"You're not telling us anything we don't know, girls. After school, Logan and I will talk to our parents, there has to be a solution to this."

The bell goes and we keep talking as we head to our respective classes. I'm hoping Jack is right and Matt sees reason.

We're in Jack's room and know we can talk without Matt interfering, he's at band practise. "We have two hours before he comes home. Mum gave me some ideas and she has spoken to both Matt and Dad, who are being stubborn. Mum threatened Matt with taking his phone away with

Dad saying he'd buy him another one. You should have seen the look on Mum's face!"

"This is the problem, your father is backing Matt giving him more power, maybe we should consider allowing them to be part of the Alliance? Not full membership, something limiting their input."

"We may have to consider this, which means getting it past the committee. We can discuss this with your parents and my mother. I hope this doesn't mean a flood of requests to become members."

I rock back and forth on his office chair. Jack, who's on his bed, is stretched out on his stomach scrolling through his phone and occasionally looking up at me. "I think we have to consider this option, you speak to your mum, I'll tackle my parents. Or we go back to my original plan where everyone thinks Matt is crazy for revealing such an unbelievable secret."

"There's risks involved with that. Have you mentioned this idea to anyone?"

"Apart from Als and Chloe, no. I'll bring it up to my parents when I talk to them about the limited membership thing."

"Sounds good, I'll talk to my mum too. Now, how about a game? I'm over talking about my stupid brother." I laugh and say yes.

It's the end of the week before I can speak to both my parents together. We're all relaxing in the lounge, it's a balmy night and the fan whirs in the corner being inefficient at cooling us. I'm chewing on an ice block, the icy sweetness cooling me. Mum and Dad are both drinking iced tea.

Explaining the situation to them, they are both horrified that Matt is causing this problem. "Getting the committee to agree to having non-magicals as members is almost impossible. There may be a slight chance it might happen, but it would take a hell of a lot of talking and convincing. On the other hand, making Matt look crazy could work. Not that I like this idea any better, but something needs to be done. How close is he to spilling our secret?"

"Oh very close, Dad. So you think letting him tell everyone will have the same effect as when his father did the same thing?"

"Yes, there are more people who think magic is a load of codswallop and doesn't exist. The few that do believe in it, well, we can use the forgetting spell on them. Remember we told you the story of Leafia and how she had to use this spell on thousands of people and it worked."

"Ah ha. Well, you need to talk to Jack's mother, he's speaking to her right now too."

"We're seeing Hannah and Noel tomorrow at the school, we're part of the fete committee for next year. We can hint to Hannah what we think is best going forward."

I've finished the ice block and am gnawing on the stick. "Oh, ok." Next year I'm in Year 11, my second last year at high school.

"Year 11 coming up for you all, any ideas of subjects you'll do for the HSC? Which will lead you into a career."

Did Dad just read my mind? I haven't even thought about our final exams in Year 12, which we start working on in semester 4 of Year 11. "Umm, I have to decide in the next two weeks. Maybe something to do with computers, the computer sciences look interesting."

They look at each other and smile. I guess I've been given the tick of approval.

It happens on the last day of school. Matt opens his big

mouth. He spreads our secret all over social media, although this isn't a big issue because his following is small. He probably has more reach with everyone gossiping about it.

Before long, people are laughing at him, sending him messages on the socials to stop being an idiot, and giving him heaps as he walks out of the school gate. What we thought would happen is happening.

I almost feel sorry for him but he was warned.

Jack walks up to me smiling like the Cheshire Cat, "He didn't listen and now he's paying for it. What a loser."

"It'll blow over by the time we're back at school next year, no one will remember."

"Yeah, but the next few weeks will be brutal. He's lucky school has finished because he can lay low. He'll only have to deal with online stuff."

The girls join us and we start walking to the shopping centre for a celebration milkshake, both for the end of school and Matt being an idiot

CHAPTER 23

LOGAN
Bullying Gets Technical

We're at the park for a geek group meeting. Many of us have been targeted with disgusting taunts and messages from Donovan and Parker. They are denying sending them as the messages are not sent from their phones, so we're suspecting they are using AI tools to write these bullying messages and sending even more disgusting images. This has us all frightened because even though the two of them have finished school they have found a way to still target us.

"So much for enjoying our summer holidays." I look around as the other geeks murmur in agreement. "Just when we thought we were rid of them, AI has given them more power. Manuel, is your sister ok? They were particularly brutal to her and her friends."

He stands up from sitting on the grass, which is cooler than sitting at the BBQ table that is in full sun. "She's having counselling and doing ok, I guess. The images sent to her phone were handed over to the police, they are investigating. I don't think we'll have to put up with this type of bullying for long. Both my sister and I told the cops who we suspected."

"That's fantastic. Hopefully the police can find out whether it was Donovan and Parker who sent such hateful stuff. Did any of you miss out?"

"I didn't receive anything," answers Aaron, "but I have a new phone, so maybe they haven't been able to get my new number yet." A few others say they hadn't either. It seems the messages were sent out randomly.

We continue talking about how to help each other if we receive more of these types of messages and images. "We have to reach out to each other and talk about how this type of bullying affects us. Don't keep this to yourselves, we need to give the police as much information as possible. And if they find out it is Donovan and Parker, then it will be interesting to see the punishment they receive."

Everyone agrees it will be the best feeling, seeing those two punished for this awful form of bullying. Who knew they could stoop any lower? Wasn't it enough they targeted us all at school? Why aren't they moving on with their lives?

After we finish with our meeting, some of us are heading to the movies, while others head home, satisfied help is on its way.

The four of us, Manuel, Aaron, Jack and I, are coming out of the movie theatre when we spot Donovan and Parker. The two heavyweights are dressed in denim jackets, looking ridiculous in the January heat. They clock us and head our way.

"Stay calm boys, they won't do anything too stupid with

all these people around. The shopping centre is buzzing with shoppers buying up big at the new year sales.

"Look at you pretty boys out on a double date," says Donovan with a swagger he thinks makes him look cool. It doesn't, he looks wobbly and drunk. I snicker stifling a laugh.

I try to defuse the situation keeping my voice amicable, "How's life treating you both now school is over?"

"None of you f'in' business, ya wanker. Now, spill out your pockets, Parker and I are hangry."

"Sorry, but I spent the last of my Christmas money on the movie. Got nothing to give."

"Well I know that's bullshit, Jacky boy. You others got anything to say?"

Manuel and Aaron shift uncomfortably so I speak for them. "Yep, same with all of us. Can't help you two today, sorry."

The four of us look around and it's suddenly quiet outside the movie theatre. Everyone has gone into the shopping centre or the café.

"Listen, hand over some money or you'll feel it from both of us." Donovan's face is red with anger, the sweat glistening on his forehead.

"How can we give you what we don't have?" I give a mock laugh and look at my friends, who all smile nervously too.

"Ever heard of an ATM? Go get some cash, all of you." Donovan is screaming at us now, a few people looking over but avoiding us.

I think on my feet and say, "So we don't have any trouble, I'll go grab some. It's been ages since I used an ATM, but I'm sure I remember how to use one."

"Shut up and get on with it. You three, we're watching

you." Both Donovan and Parker stand their ground as I walk away ready to transform.

"We know it was you two who sent those messages and images. You know the police have them now."

Parker looks at Donovan who quickly laughs Jack's comment off, "Yeah right, and the police are going to care about a few geeks whinging that their phones have been hacked. It wasn't us, we have nothin' to worry about."

I hear Donovan say this as I head for his ankles and pee on his left one. "What the hell. Shit!"

As he and Parker are distracted by me as the Maine Coon, Jack heads off to transform and comes back yapping and nipping at Parker's ankles. This brings a crowd of people to watch, the laughter filling the area in front of the movie theatre.

"Disgusting. You mangy cat. What a stink." Donovan shakes his ankle making the crowd laugh louder. Someone from the crowd calls out, "Frightened by a cat, hey Dono?" Meanwhile, Parker, who is still scared of Jack the Jack Russel, shakes his leg trying to loosen the dog's grip, but Jack rips into his sock even harder.

The next thing everyone hears is an almighty screech coming from me, the Maine Coon. Donovan has unleashed a punch into my cat face completely splitting my eye. Jack lets go of Parker's leg and runs over to me where I landed near a concrete planter box.

Manuel and Aaron who had sparked into action video-ing, stop filming. "We're sending these videos to the police, this is harassment and violence," says Manuel. With this Donovan and Parker flee the scene, probably thinking that if the police do turn up, they will be interrogated not just about what happened here, but also about the messages and images. The police have been investigating long enough and probably have information on who sent them.

Jack, transformed to his human self, is holding me with caution. "Quick, let's get this cat to a vet, his eye looks very damaged." Someone from the crowd offers to help, it's the gardener from our school. The three boys squeeze into his Ute with Jack still holding onto me and assuring me I am going to be ok.

Jack was asked to go down to the police station to make a witness statement and asked me to go with him. When the police arrived at the shopping centre, Donovan and Parker were long gone, but Jack was asked to go to the station after seeing the vet. Manuel and Aaron had left to go home, not wanting to be involved any further other than handing in the videos they took.

The Glenndale police station is a nondescript building, the front is blonde brick with a small aluminium window on the left and an aging timber front door. I don't know what I was expecting it to look like, I had a vision of a grander building. This idea probably comes from watching American crime shows. There was no Australian flag flapping in front of this station.

After entering, we give our names to the uniformed officer standing behind the steel grill who asks us to take a seat. We can see a mess of desks, chairs and computers to the left of us, many of them empty. It's after four, so who knows where the officers who fill these desks are? My eye aches, the pain killers starting to wear off. Luckily, the damage looked worse when I was a cat, but I received two stitches under my right eye that is now swollen, blue with bruising and I can see through a slight slit. Under my left eye I was a little bruised but I can see out of it. I must have groaned because Jack asks how I am.

"Bit sore, but ok. I hope this doesn't take too long, I really want to be home."

"Yeah, it's been a hell of a day. We would've been home hours ago if it wasn't for those idiots."

"I honestly thought they'd go away after leaving school, this sucks."

"I know. But with the police involved now we may get our revenge."

"I hope so, Jack."

Before I could say more, a uniformed officer walks towards us. "Good afternoon, Jack is it?" She holds out her hand for him to shake. "I'm Constable Jane Pathe."

"Hello," replies Jack, "and this is my friend Logan. He's here supporting me."

"Hello, Logan. That's quite a bruiser you have there."

"Stupid accident. Nice to meet you Constable." I offer my hand for her to shake.

"Ok, follow me please. I'm taking you to an interrogation room, but please don't be alarmed, you are not in trouble. It's the only room where we won't be interrupted. I will be recording you for your witness statements, but again, there is nothing to worry about." We both follow her giving each other a look of concern. With me feeling grateful she didn't ask anything more about my injuries.

The room is stark with high windows, a bright fluorescent light, a simple white desk with two chairs on either side. Constable Jane asks us to take a seat offering us a drink. We both decline not wanting to prolong this.

Once we're settled, she sits opposite us, places her phone in front of her clicking record. "We've checked the videos your friends gave us and it seems you four were intimidated by those two. None of you caused them to react in that way. What I'm curious about is where did the cat and dog come from? Are they your pets?"

Jack allows me to answer. "No, they're probably a couple of ferals. We've seen them around our school occasionally."

"Right. My daughter has commented on seeing them too. You go to Glenndale High then?"

"Yes."

"Do you both know the boys who were harassing you?" We both nod. "They have bothered you before?"

"Occasionally at school. Not just us." I'm keeping my responses short not wanting to say something that may get us into trouble.

"Relax, Logan. I'm trying to help you, the more information you can give us, the more we can get down to knowing why you were targeted." She continues, "My Sergeant who was on the scene explained that those two, Donovan Schmidt and Parker Bennet, are suspected of sending out bullying messages, is this correct?"

Jack and I look at each other, there is no reason for us to deny this. Jack answers, "There is a group of us who have received messages and disgusting images that we think are AI generated by them. One girl in particular was badly traumatised. Most of us are frightened."

"I'm sorry to hear that. These are serious allegations and if proven guilty, they can be charged under our Telecommunications Offences Act. However, it can take some time before we find the IP addresses and figure out who owns them. If this is the first time these two have done this, they may have left a trail, making it easier to us to find them." We both give a sigh of relief.

"Well, thank you both for talking to me. If you think of

anything else, or if any of your friends do, please let me know." She hands over her card to each of us, "I'll organise a car to take you both home. Also, please be vigilant, these two could target you and your friends again."

We thank her and sit on the chairs we sat on when we came in while we wait for our driver. Both of us know it isn't the end, Donovan and Parker will keep going.

LOGAN
New Year, New Bullies

Jack and I are in Year 11 along with Manuel, Aaron, and Tahlia. Chloe and Georgia are in Year 10. We're all excited about our last years at school and are seated in our usual place under the shade of the Jacaranda.

Jack is thinking about the Higher School Certificate (HSC) after we were briefed on it a few days ago. "There is so much work. We even have to do work during the holidays."

"You have to keep up with the work, that's all. There is no way around it if you want to go to university," I answer. "I might take a gap year though, do some travelling."

"Your job filling shelves gives you enough money to travel?"

"Not really, but I have another two years to save, Jack. Still, I haven't decided yet. What about you?"

"A bit like you, undecided. I'm looking at engineering

and computer courses now. But who knows, I might join you on a gap year."

"That'd be cool."

At the end of this first week, we meet at the side gate ready to walk home together. The three of us are on our phones before we start walking. I'm the first to see the news report.

Breaking News

Glenndale Police has given us the latest on their work with cyber-bullying, which is on the rise throughout our younger community.

Donovan Schmidt and Parker Bennet, both 18, have been found guilty of sending damaging and bullying messages and graphic images to members of the Glenndale school community.

"Are you guys reading this?" I turn my phone towards them, "Donovan and Parker are going to be doing time. What the fu ..."

"Yep, reading it now. Wow, how sweet is revenge? This is the best news," smiles Jack.

"It is. And the scar under my eye reminds me of what Donovan did. They obviously left a trail like the Constable told us."

Jack laughs, "Typical right? They wouldn't be smart enough to cover their tracks. I'm so pumped, I hope they get life." We all laugh knowing that won't happen but secretly wish it would. We head home talking about this great news enjoying the fact those bullies will receive what they deserve.

The next week our school is buzzing with the news that Donovan and Parker were given a two-year sentence each.

Manuel and Aaron come over and talk to us at our lockers before we have to go to class.

Aaron slaps me on the back, "Looks like we did it, hey Logan? I'm sure Manuel's and my videos helped?"

I laugh at his enthusiasm, "I'm sure they did in showing that they are bullies. But it's the police we have to thank for finding out who sent those messages."

"True," says Manuel, "but I like the idea we were able to give them evidence of them bullying us."

"We did help, all of us." I close my locker to see Miller and Scarlett glaring at us. I look around to find only Jack is standing with me, Manuel and Aaron had already headed to class.

"Are you pleased with yourselves?" asks Miller, "ruining two lives because you were scared wimps."

Jack scoffs, "How is this our fault. They did it to themselves by going too far with the AI stuff. They should have moved on after leaving school."

"Come on, Jack, we need to get to class. Ladies ...," I say as we leave. They stand with their arms folded, Miller giving us the finger when we turn back to see if they have left.

Lunchtime comes around and we're in our usual spot sucking on ice blocks trying to keep cool. Miller and Scarlett approach us with two boys we don't know.

"These are the wimps we were telling you about. Wimps, meet Cole and Maddox, they're mates of Donovan and Parker."

I look at the two boys who up close I can now see are men, not boys. They are definitely not students. What the hell are they doing on school grounds?

"We're not pleased about our friends being given prison

sentences. We hear you lot had a part in this happening." This from the dark haired one with a side buzz-cut and thick curls on top. He has no neck and is as buff as they come. The veins popping out of his muscles are frightening. The one next to him, a smaller version of the same only his curls are tipped blonde, punches one hand into the other. To say he is menacing is an understatement.

"Not sure where you got that from," I say hoping this doesn't escalate. It's only day two of school and we're being bullied yet again.

"Don't bullshit us, Logan." *How did he know my name? This is not good.* "We know you went to the police station."

"What is going on here?" A teacher has walked up. "You two don't belong here?" she says nodding her head towards the two men.

"We're caring brothers bringing our sisters their lunch. We'll be on our way now. See you later sis." The one I assume is Cole smiles at the teacher and they both walk towards the school side gate.

"Miller and Scarlett, go to the principal's office and explain how your 'brothers' came to be on school grounds without permission. The rest of you, back to class."

"Thanks, Miss." I say this with a sigh of relief. We would have been no match for those two. Heading to class I'm hoping this was a one-off visit from them.

Saturday night and we're at the bowling alley celebrating Als' 18th birthday. Chloe and Als against Jack and me. And they're beating our arses off.

"Another strike! Do you have a tracker in that ball Als?" Jack laughs as he places his fingers in the three holes of the black ball.

"It's my birthday, I have a right to win." We all fall

about laughing, we've had a great night. "Thanks for this by the way, I know it was short notice. I didn't want anything big with all the work I have to do for university."

"This is fun," says Chloe, "and you have to celebrate your 18th, you're an adult now."

"I know, how bizarre. I've had my first taste of beer too, two nights ago on my actual birthday. Dad said he'd rather see me drinking at home to get a taste for it."

"And how was it?" asks Jack throwing the ball down the aisle.

"A bit sour, I'm not sure I like it." She stops. "Woah, you got a strike."

"Ha, that's the secret, don't concentrate on what you're doing."

"Yeah, but we still beat you. Come on, let's go, game's over."

After taking off our bowling shoes and handing them back to the attendant, we head out to Als' car. Well, her father's car. But as we head to the black Mercedes, Cole and Maddox appear from behind it.

"Did you wimps enjoy bowling tonight?" The night sky has high clouds that are filtering through the full moon giving the evening an eerie glow. Their faces in shadow.

Als has the car keys in her hand. And her phone. She clicks it open. "I'm ready to film this."

"Oh, we have a brave one here. Don't worry wimp girl, we're here delivering a message, that's all." It's Cole speaking again, Maddox doesn't seem to do any of the talking. "Our friends you put in prison will be out soon for good behaviour and they're looking forward to seeing you again."

This is crazy, they've only been in prison six months. Before any of us can answer, they walk towards a dilapidated Ute on the other side of the car park, Cole turns around and walks backwards, "We'll be in touch when they're out."

We watch on as they leave, all of us stunned. Then we all climb into the Mercedes. We're dumbstruck as Als drives us home.

Jack and I are back at the police station talking with Constable Jane. This time with our dads for support. She is explaining there is not much she can do. "I'm sorry, but they have been model prisoners, helping out and keeping their noses clean. Given their age and the fact they have apologised for their actions, their parole officer has asked for them to be given early release with some home detention."

"This is crazy, they were given two years."

"They were Logan, but with good behaviour and a successful appeal, they will be released this October."

"And there is nothing to stop that?" asks my father.

"I'm afraid not. However, if they do cause you trouble, let us know right away. Don't wait until they cause more problems with their intimidation."

"I don't believe this. They are known now as bullies and can get away with it." Jack shakes his head. Noel places his hand on his shoulder.

"The fact we know this will go against them. We will always keep an eye on what they are doing."

I explain about the other two, Cole and Maddox, who are years older than Donovan and Parker. "They are like protectors or something."

"It's probable your bullies are part of a gang, this happens often once school is behind them. They become part of a gang and commit minor crimes. Many of them end up back in prison."

"And that's where they should stay," says Noel.

"Mr Sterling and Mr Shipley, I understand your concerns and how you want to protect your boys, but please don't take this into your own hands, let us know before anyone gets hurt." Constable Jane hands out two more cards to our dads. "Thank you for coming, we're here when you need us."

As we're walking back to Noel's car, he asks, "Can't you guys use your magic to solve this?"

My dad answers, "If it escalates, we may need to, but for now we have to wait until October and see what happens. I don't want Logan or anyone else getting injured again, his scar under his eye has only just dried out and is not as visible."

Noel nods, "Yeah, those idiots need to learn a lesson before their lives are ruined," he says, "I know I learned my lesson before it was too late." He puts the key in the ignition and we head home.

CHAPTER 25

LOGAN

Magic is Required

October arrives and our nerves are on edge. I keep looking behind my shoulder wondering if the bullies, four of them now, are following me. We try and stay in groups when we're out of school for safety, but we're still scared.

My father has asked the other magicals to help if they are needed, many of whom are willing and waiting for the signal. They are horrified it has come to this and how the police have basically no power to keep the offenders in prison. "What do you think we can use on them? They are gang members now and even more dangerous," he had asked the committee.

Their answers were encouraging but we were still hoping we could ask the bullies to see reason, at least that's what our families are hoping. Us geeks are not so sure.

As much as possible, our dads are with us if we have to go out at night. I feel like a kid again but know it's better this way. Donovan and Parker have been seen around the shopping centre a few times but haven't caused any problems. This is what we're discussing as we're leaving the school grounds ready for another vigilant weekend.

"We have to wait here, my dad will be here soon."

"We know, Logan. Stop babying us."

"Sorry, Als. I'm so on edge, my body and mind are on high alert."

"It's ok, I get it. We're all frightened. It's like a ticking time bomb."

My dad arrives and we all pile into the car. "Ok, who needs to go where?"

I don't have any after school activities but Jack needs to go to the gym, Als is going home but has a tutor coming over and Chloe has a dance class. "Have you two organised a pickup?" he asks looking at Jack and Chloe. They both answer yes. "Good, let's get on with it then."

This is our life now, we are not allowed to be on our own, we're older but still being ferried everywhere by our parents to keep us safe, and the other geeks are also staying vigilant.

The geek group is having a meeting at the park. Even though bullying at school has eased, threats from Cole and Maddox keep coming in the form of cyber-attacks. We report anything we receive to the police who a compiling evidence on this gang. "Keep wary of them but don't engage," Constable Jane had warned us.

Our fathers, Jack's and mine have gone to run errands coming back in less than an hour. We can achieve a lot in that time.

I wait until everyone settles down, many are catching up after the holidays. "Right, thanks for coming everyone.

Would each of you please give us a rundown of anything that has happened to you, we'll start with you Manuel."

To my surprise not as many people have been targeted as I thought. "Thanks, it seems only a few of you have been targeted this time, which can be a good thing. Maybe Cole and Maddox are losing interest?"

"Not likely," says Jack, "They're waiting to hear from Donovan and Parker. They've only been out a few days so are probably lying low so they don't attract attention. The police will be watching them." I nod as I hadn't thought of that, things could get worse now those two are out of prison. And way too early in my opinion.

The meeting is over early, so everyone heads back home, mostly by parents picking them up. Jack and I are waiting for our dads who should be here any minute. We're sitting at the BBQ table when the four of them turn up. Donovan, Parker, Cole and Maddox are behind us. "Well, the two lovebirds are on their own, how sweet." There is no mistaking Donovan's voice.

Jack and I turn as we stand up. "What the hell are you doing out Donovan? Aren't you and Parker on house arrest?"

"We are," he says proudly showing his ankle bracelet, "this little baby monitors where I go and I'm not out of range yet. Nice of you two to have your meetings local, it helps us out a lot." He smirks while indicating to the other three.

"Listen Donovan, don't do anything stupid or you'll end up back in prison."

"Jacky, still fiery I see. But you two have to pay for getting Parker and meself locked up. We're not letting you get away with that now are we?"

"Listen to Jack, you're asking for trouble." I keep talking

as I see our dads walking up behind the four bullies, wanting to keep them focused on Jack and me.

Donovan's face turns bitter with rage and he hurls verbal abuse at us. His violent swearing is intimidating.

Jack's father walks around to join Jack and I as Donovan keeps ranting. "Who the hell are you?"

Noel smiles and is restrained. He shows a calmness I didn't know he had. "Gentlemen, I've been where you are, I too was a bully during my school years. Now, I can see two of you have not long been out of school, but I'm sure your bullying days didn't start after you left school. So, now we have established who and what you are, I kindly ask you to leave."

"Oh, you kindly ask us to leave, do you? How polite of you to ask." Donovan places a fake smile on his face, "whoever you are you have no place here. This is between meself, my friend here, Parker and the other two standing behind us." He takes a couple of steps forward, Parker joining him. Cole and Maddox stay back.

"Don't even think about coming any closer. Donovan, is it? I'm Noel, Jack's father. If you do anything to hurt these two boys again, believe me you will regret it." Donovan flicks his wrist and releases a pocketknife. "Woah, put that away."

My dad joins us, he had been waiting behind the bullies waiting to see what was going to happen. "Donovan, you and I have spoken before. Put that knife away as Noel has asked. We can talk this through."

Laughter comes from the four of them.

"Shipley, right? You're Logan's dad." My dad nods. "How nice of you to suggest we can talk, but this isn't a mother's group, we're not here to chat. Parker and me spent 9 months in gaol, in f'ing prison! And you want to talk?" His laughter bellows out of him as he points the knife closer to us.

I am fumbling to reach my phone in my pocket but my hands are slippery with sweat, my whole body is on high alert. Donovan and Parker are scary enough let alone with those two standing behind them. I press numbers on the phone hoping I've pressed triple o. I don't think I've succeeded.

The sun is setting adding an eerie glow to the park and it's cooler. I shiver despite sweating. We have to do something. I whisper to Dad, "We need to transform. Or can you do that magic we talked about?"

"Want to share that with all of us, Logan? You sharin' secrets over there?" When I don't answer, Donovan lunges at my dad narrowly missing him. Dad starts saying something under his breath and I know it's magic. He's using the paralysing incantation as he moves towards the four bullies.

"What are you mumbling?" Donovan's voice is shaky, the other three step back away from him. Donovan is the first to be paralysed to the spot. Dad walks towards the other three and targets Parker. He is frozen too. Cole and Maddox are stopped in their tracks trying to run away. The whole scene is hilarious and the only things moving on the four of them is their panicked eyes.

"Now gentlemen," says my dad placing himself on the table. "We're going to leave you like this all night and let the mozzies eat you alive. We all know how bad the mosquitos are with all this bushland around. But first, I want to show you how your life is going to pan out because of the stupidity you are showing in bullying Logan and Jack." As he talks a mirage-like shadow opens up in between two trees. It shows a scene with the four of them, Cole and Maddox are lying injured on the blood-soaked dirt, Donovan and Parker are being handcuffed by police.

Their eyes flinch with fear. We can see Donovan trying to speak, his mouth twitching.

"This is your life if you keep following this path of bullying and crime. Don't think this is a joke, it's not. Now, it's late so we'll leave you to keep watching how this scenario pans out for you. Enjoy your evening gentlemen." Dad nods to us to head to the car looking pleased with himself, this new power he has to conjure life scenarios has come in handy.

As we sit in the car and Noel drives, I thank them for helping us. "That was incredible, Dad. I've never seen Donovan and Parker so scared. Will the four of them really be there all night?"

"They sure will. The paralysing spell takes twelve hours to wear off. I have to say, I enjoyed seeing their fear and I hope this changes their ways."

Noel look towards my father, "I hope you're right, Edward. It is an amazing power you have there, but it remains to be seen if it is enough to scare them. Especially Cole and Maddox, they have been in a gang for years now."

I look at Jack who is as stunned as I am, we were both hoping this was going to teach the bullies a lesson once and for all.

The End

More to come in Book Three.

ACKNOWLEDGMENTS

When I wrote Book One of this magical story I didn't know there was more to it but my readers wanted more. Edward's Cat, The Rise of the Kittens. And a Dog, is Book Two of this trilogy. At least right now I see a trilogy, but who knows? Will there be more to the magicals stories?

The idea for Edward's story started as a writing prompt for one of my writing groups, *Write on Water*. It is thanks to the other authors in the group that this story is now published. I thank you, especially those who helped with reading and editing, your suggested changes were invaluable.

I recommend any author, especially emerging ones to join a local writing group. Follow them on socials too. The knowledge and camaraderie you receive is so helpful. Our meetings are always full of facts, fun and sometimes food. We encourage each other and together we can achieve anything in this writing and publishing gig.

As always, thanks to my colleague and friend, Mark Drolc, for designing my book covers. You are patient, put up with my changes, and always enhance my ideas. A big thanks to you, Mark.

Thanks also to my beta readers, your feedback always makes my stories better. Of course, thanks go to my family, my friends and my colleagues. You're all behind me encouraging my creativity, and for this I'm grateful.

ABOUT THE AUTHOR

Maria has made a career of using words to communicate. Working at a TV station, her first paid job, nurtured Maria's love of words. A move to Sydney to study Communications gave her the opportunity to work with advertising & public relations agencies, corporate companies and newspapers. She has written PR, ads and newsletters for products from food to jewellery, fashion and interiors as well as garden and building products. When she is not writing corporate communications or as a Senior Reviewer for the online site, Weekend Notes, she works on her short stories and novels.

Her first published story, **The Studio** is a crime short story. **Xenure Station: A Billion Light Years** is Maria's second short story. Both are available as eBooks wherever books are sold online.

The Decision They Made, Maria's debut novel and her other books are available on her website – www.mari-apfrino.com. Buy these books as eBooks or print. **Weaving Words**, an anthology Maria collaborated on, is also available as an audiobook. Maria contributed two short stories to this anthology along with eight other authors.